IF THESE STREETS COULD TALK

IF THESE STREETS COULD TALK

NYWC
New York Writers Coalition

NY WRITERS COALITION PRESS
BROOKLYN ~ 2006

If These Streets Could Talk
© 2006 NY Writers Coalition Inc.

ALL RIGHTS RESERVED. Upon publication, copyright to individual works
returns to the authors.

Published by NY Writers Coalition Press, a division of NY Writers Coalition Inc.,
Brooklyn, New York. For orders and information, please contact

NY Writers Coalition Inc.
80 Hanson Place #603
Brooklyn, NY 11217
(718) 398-2883
info@nywriterscoalition.org
www.nywriterscoalition.org

ISBN 0-9787794-0-1
Printed and bound in the USA.
Library of Congress Control Number: 2006930678

Book & cover design by Christian Peet, Tarpaulin Sky Design (www.tarpaulinsky.com)
Title font: Downcome, by Eduardo Recife, Misprinted Type.
Text font: Adobe Garamonde Pro

CONTENTS

THE OPPOSITE OF LONELINESS

GO UPWARDS OR BE THROWN DOWN

KIM HAS A FUR NOSE

THE SUN SHINES ON THIS SIDE OF THE STREET

PREFACE

About New York Writers Coalition (NYWC)

NYWC, a 501(c)3 not-for-profit organization, creates opportunities for formerly voiceless members of society to be heard through the art of writing. We provide free, unique and powerful creative writing workshops throughout New York City for people from groups that have been historically deprived of voice in our society, including at-risk youth, adult residents of supportive housing, the formerly incarcerated, seniors and others.

NYWC is one of the largest community-based writing organizations in the country. Each year, we conduct hundreds of workshop sessions at approximately 25 locations, creating ongoing writing communities throughout the city. We've published numerous anthologies of writing by our workshop members as well as **Plum Biscuit**, an online literary magazine edited by our workshop members. NYWC also operates the **Writing Aloud** reading series, a monthly event featuring members of our workshops reading alongside established authors; **Write Makes Might**, an annual marathon reading by our workshop members; and is a partner in the annual **Fort Greene Park Summer Literary Festival**, a series of writing workshops for young people culminating in a reading by the young writers with literary icons such as Amiri Baraka, Jhumpa Lahiri, Sonia Sanchez and Sapphire. Workshop participants have had poems, stories and plays published and performed. Others have read their writing on NPR's *All Things Considered,* WNYC's *Brian Lehrer Show* and WBAI's *Global Movements, Urban Struggles.*

As a small, grassroots organization, NYWC relies on the generous support of those dedicated to getting the voices heard of those who have been silenced. Thanks go to our foundation, government and corporate supporters, including Brooklyn Arts Council, Con Edison, Cowan Slavin Foundation, Emmanuel Baptist Church, Hot Topic Foundation, Independence Community Foundation, Kalliopeia Foundation, NYC Council Member Letitia James, NYC Department of Cultural Affairs, New York State Council For The Arts, Petra Foundation, Pinkerton Foundation, Puffin Foundation, Time Warner's Youth Media and Arts Fund and Union Square Arts Awards. Special thanks is due to Andrea Weinstein of Cowan Slavin Foundation for her belief in our work before anyone else supported us and to Stuart Post of Independence Community Foundation for his tireless championing of NYWC. Thanks also to our program partner Isis Sapp-Grant of the Youth Empowerment Mission for her many words of wisdom and encouragement as NYWC grew from being operated out of a bedroom corner into a powerful force throughout New York City.

We also rely heavily on the support of many individuals. Our workshop leaders have volunteered thousands of hours because they believe in giving back to their communities. Many others have made financial contributions and attended our events. Thanks go to NYWC Program Director Deborah Clearman for doing all three of these things (volunteering, making donations and attending everything!). In addition, our Board of Directors, Abeni Crooms, Frank Haberle, Nancy Weber, and Executive Director Aaron Zimmerman, have stewarded us through the joyous struggle to keep our vital work going. To find out how you can support us by becoming a member or participating in our annual Write-A-Thon, please visit our website at **www.nywriterscoalition.org**.

This anthology contains some of the writing created by our workshop members from our inception in May 2002 through August 2005. Most of the writing in this book was created during our workshops, gathered in a room with other writers. Participants from NYWC's first three years were invited to submit work of their own choosing, and writing from everyone that submitted is included. Writers made all editorial decisions about their own work. The editorial committee, made up of NYWC staff and volunteers, read all submitted work and when appropriate, selected writing from a range of pieces by a given writer. We take great pride in our efforts to be inclusive, and to present the writers' work in their true, beautiful voices.

NYWC Workshop Sites and Leaders

Writers included in this anthology participated in workshops at one of the below listed locations.

The Aurora: Supportive housing operated by The Actor's Fund and Common Ground. Workshop Leader: Melanie O'Harra.

Blossom Program For Girls: A program for teenage girls at high risk of gang involvement in Bedford-Stuyvesant, Brooklyn, operated by Youth Empowerment Mission Inc. Workshop Leaders: Julia Morris, Susanna Schrobsdorff.

Community House: A supportive housing community in Park Slope, Brooklyn operated by Community House/Prospect Park Y. Workshop Leaders: Rob Darnell, Ivy Weiskopf.

Fort Greene Park Summer Literary Festival: Two summer-long, outdoor writing workshops for young people in Fort Greene, Brooklyn. Workshop Leaders: Angeli Rasbury, Julia Schaffer, Ivy Weiskopf.

Gilda's Club: A non-residential support community for people affected by cancer and their families and friends. Workshop Leaders: Shaina Feinberg, Beth Sandor.

Hopper Home: Housing for women as an alternative to incarceration, operated by Women's Prison Association & Home. Workshop Leader: Madeleine George.

The Prince George: Supportive housing operated by Common Ground and Center for Urban Community Services. Workshop Leader: Nancy Weber.

Queens Public Library, Broadway Branch: Workshop for kids in the diverse community of Long Island City. Workshop Leader: Julia Schaffer.

Sol Goldman Y Educational Center for Retired Adults: A program of classes for older adults, operated by The Educational Alliance. Workshop Leader: Deborah Clearman.

Stay N Out/Serendipity: Residence in Bedford-Stuyvesant, Brooklyn, for formerly incarcerated women seeking substance abuse treatment, operated by NY Therapeutic Communities. Workshop Leader: Erik Rhey.

St. Francis Residences: Housing and support services to homeless men and women with a history of chronic mental illness operated by the Catholic Charities/St. Francis Friends of The Poor. Workshop Leader: Shaina Feinberg.

World Trade Center Survivors Network: A support and advocacy group for survivors of the attacks on the World Trade Center. Workshop Leader: Aaron Zimmerman.

INTRODUCTION

If These Streets Could Talk

What we were most struck by when we first read the pieces that comprise this Anthology is how much they reflect what you might hear if these many and various New York streets could talk: reflections of identity from a seven-year-old Chinese-American girl living in Queens, an immigrant's tale of leaving Cuba in 1971, a story describing the horrors of being homeless in 1980s Manhattan, a poem evoking the terror of an AIDS victim, a description of the loveliness of eating a patisserie's brioche, a poem exposing a World Trade Center survivor's daily struggles.

These stories and poems are New York.

But what does that mean? It's hard to think of New York City as a community. With over eight million residents spanning every age, race, and economic level, it is difficult to imagine what might bind us all together.

The pages that follow answer this question. The writers who contributed to this Anthology come from diverse backgrounds, which their unique voices reflect. Their stories and poems touch upon a wide variety of themes. But what the people whose work fill these pages have in common is that they have all discovered the power of their own voice, of putting a pen to paper and telling a story, in their own words. In doing so, their pieces don't only tell their individual perspectives on struggle and triumph, love and hate, despair and hope, but also illustrate universal questions and answers concerning what it is to be human.

In this way, we like to think of this book as a community within itself. A collection of New York voices not often heard from. Perhaps reading the pieces to follow will inspire you to write your own story, or will give you insight as to what it might be like to walk in someone else's shoes. Regardless, we hope you enjoy reading it as much as we have.

Deborah Clearman
Joshua Bolotsky
Rebecca Strauss
Raina Wallens

I AM FROM BIG WHITE DUMPLINGS

PRETTY

BY CINDY LEI, AGE 7

I am from New York City
I am from brushes with daisies
I am from big white dumplings with things inside
I am from long pink dresses that I wear for dances.
I feel excited when I am wearing the pink dress.
I am from fudge
I am from congratulations and happy birthday.
I am from presents, medium-sized in a blue box
with a pink ribbon.
I am from fresh air.

I am from quickly-spoken Chinese.
I am from the stories I write, stories with problems.
I am from little and big sisters.
I am from Chinatown where there are interesting signs
and English-speaking people can't understand.

I AM FROM

BY PETER MILLER

I am from New York's World Trade Center, the
   belching clouds of ashes and dust.
Expelled like a thing that scurries. I am from the
   ruins with all my parts intact.
Living to move on and get on, despite the images of
   Armageddon and that special smell.

I am From-mer, traveling all over the world on five
   dollars a day.

I am fromage with very special smells.

I am frommenting wine weaving through barrels and
   bottles to your tables.

I am from some other place pretending to fit in. It's
   easy once you get the hang of it.

I AM FROM

BY JAHNIA T. MARK, AGE 7

I am from marble cakes that are tasty
in a big kitchen with a clock
and chocolate lollipops my mother makes
yellow, white, brown, red and purple,
different shapes of lollipops.

I AM FROM

BY LORIE BARNES

I am from scents and savories,
from vodka and brandy and Benedictine,
from losing and luminescence
and caramel pie.
Yellow roses made me grin, along with slides
down a marble staircase
with two marble-frozen lovers
embracing by the stairs.
I am inching, tummy first, down another staircase
seeking elderly aunts,
then reciting the Twenty-Third Psalm from memory.
My pigtails are tied; so is my tongue.
There is gum in them.
Curling irons and Shirley Temple are my nemeses.
I smash a doll over a terrace to the street.

Now, I waver and shiver, trying to triumph.

WHERE I'M FROM

BY SYDNE BROWN, AGE 7

I am from Jamaica where the beautiful south is. I am from the doctor's office where the doctors take a two-hour lunch. I am from fast food because fast is great.

THE MUSE

BY LORIE BARNES

Alone I floated to this plane;
My mother said she knew slight pain.
I caught a wave within the womb,
And I shall ride it to my tomb.
I swear that I remember still
The taste that was my suckling will,
That quenched my thirst upon the breast,
And gave me warmth, welcome, and rest.

When I was drei, trois, tres and three
After three hundred lives of me,
From far millenniums ago
I knew the things that I would know.
I spoke at one, I mused at night,
Precocious words I could not write.
And I was told that more than once
At three, I spoke of "sibilance."

At seventy-four I seek it yet,
For it is still a pirouette
That spins around from age to age,
And disappears somewhere backstage.
I have a sybil, I am sure,
And once embraced she will endure;
She is the muse one day I'll find,
Just out of reach, just out of mind.

I LIKE MYSTERY

BY TIFFANY WONG, AGE 8

I like mystery
But I hate history!

Three fools
In a pool

I wish a wizard
Could blow away a blizzard

Fairies
Are hairy

Gravity
Gives you cavities

Summer is sometimes
A bummer

If you're not a bat
You are a rat

You should
Eat a shoe

Blowing makes
You growing

Ring a bell
And go to hell

Bugs
Turn into slugs

Boys eat
Toys

THINGS I WISH TO FORGET

BY ANTONIA MALDONADO

1. That I'm not very athletic.

2. Don't always eat my vegetables.

3. Don't try to run anymore, but I'm going to try some-time over the weekend.

4. That I have a whole bunch of newspapers that I should read.

5. That I have to clean my apartment.

   a) The plumber came and I have a lot of dust all over.

   a) It makes me sneeze, but I'll tackle it later today or on Saturday for sure.

   b) The plumber is cleaning my shower and I think I'll have a lot of dirt on the floors.

   b) I am a little tired today.

6. I saw Martha Stewart's show and she had all kinds of beautiful glasses and I used to have the same ones.

7. I hope to cook a big meal Sunday but I think I have forgotten something I should have bought at the vegetable shop (Garden of Eden).

8. Crock pot cooking is on the menu. I always worry that it's not going to taste good, but it always does.

9. I guess I can't believe that I am 61 years old. I feel like I am 30.

10. I forgot to take a lot of pictures on our trip to the country. I was too busy talking.

11. I need to forget all my silly notions, like the sky going to fall, or an airplane crash. I feel that I have a good memory, but I do and don't.

SHUNN THEINGI

BY SHUNN THEINGI, AGE 9

Season
Houseboat
Umbrella
Neighbor
Near the pond, fishing

The children are playing
House
Elephant in the Bronx Zoo
In the pool, people are swimming
Near the beach, full of people
Grasshopper
Ink

UNTITLED 1 (JEANNIE)

BY GABRIELLE REM

Hey, Jeannie, first I've got to tell you that I love that costume of yours. It looks so cool and comfortable. I have so many questions. How do you make yourself *poof*—into smoke—*poof* back into yourself? More importantly, show me how to blink my eyes like you do or dip my head to get things to happen, turn people into animals—though that would be giving people more credit than they deserve, unless of course you turned them into what some of them really are: asses. What did you have to do to get these powers? Where are you from? Can you give me your powers for a day? There are so many things I would like to do, imagine, be, see, experience…Then *poof*—there she went back into her bottle. She just left me hanging and then I opened my eyes and realized my mind can take me places, show me things, and let me experience all sorts of things just by the magic inside.

BRIAN LEONG

BY BRIAN LEONG, AGE 5

Banana
Rainbow
Igloo
Air
Nap

Lap
Elephant
Octopus
Nap
Giraffe

KEYHOLE TO MY WORLD

BY WESLEY MAXWELL BAYNES

Through my keyhole I can see my magnificent world. I can see my Xs which represent my thoughts and acts. The Xs also bring me fulfillment.

The next image I see through my keyhole is my bird of love. It brings me love in abundance. A love that I reflect back into the world many times over.

My next image is that of a horse. The horse represents power and stamina. I hope that the horse's power and stamina bring me a lasting life and good existence.

A house is the next image that I see. I do not own a house at present; but I will be striving for that. The power of ownership is my goal.

The next image is that of a river which represents the flow of life. Right now, it reminds that life slowly ebbs away. I would therefore have to take charge and live a good life.

WINGS-NO PASSPORT

BY JUDIE DAVID

I arrived without fanfare,
also without fortune.
Being born was my parents' idea.
They just plopped me down,
saying, "We'll give you the wings.
You fly as high as you can."
They provided me with a birth certificate
but strangely, no passport.

I found it hard to use the wings:
they just made little flips.
I flipped around until I realized
I would have to make my own passport.
I hoped it would be accepted as genuine.

I got my stamps by degrees and Degrees.
When I first started, I had trouble getting in
although less so as my stamps increased.
Once in, conditions were often not to my liking
so I wanted to get out!
My wings were flapping fabulously now,
so I soared above the fray, chuckling as I went.

Now my passport is quite filled up
With views from mountaintops

As well as subway depths,
ideas that jump me as they jump off the page,
people of varying shapes and affabilities
the great City College of New York
where I and Jonas Salk started out.
Best of all, three loves,
coming in different sizes.

One day I was flying high.
My passport fell and I was frantic.
Then I leaned back and reminisced,
grinning.

I USED TO BE, BUT NOW

BY PETER MILLER

I used to be a simple rustic farm boy
But now, I'm a sophisticated urban businessman.

Life was less complicated then.
I used to walk on dirt roads
And ride a bicycle forever.
But now, I'm all about airways and Acelas.

I used to birth lambs
And hatch chicks
And grow crops.
I used to kill varmints
And burn brush.
And shovel manure.

But now I conceive of strategic plans
And hatch political intrigue
And grow companies
And kill the competition
And burn the midnight oil
And yet, I still shovel a lot of shit!

YESTERDAY

BY LESLIE BROWN

Yesterday
I looked out of myself and saw someone
Scared
Not knowing what the possibilities of life are
Seeing flashbacks of the turmoil it can bring
But yet not uncovering what really lies beyond
It is the epitome of the ending of the struggle
The true reason for living

Yesterday
I saw a woman full of circumstance
Not caring of the world
But still cognizant of her surroundings
She sees the world different from others
It is a world unlike any other
Which is tranquil but you're still
Somewhat confused

Today
I see a woman elaborate
One full of Nubian pizzazz
Today I see me

THE OPPOSITE OF LONELINESS

LOVE

BY SHERWOOD JACOBSON

Which memory will come?
The ocean, where my mother held my hand
and led me into the water when I was a child.
Death has taken my mother.
It made her slither away.
I loved so many people.
Why were my hands so weak
as to not hold love forever?
Somewhere, there must be an unknown time,
which will catch the embers
to start the fire
to warm this cold world
which does not understand my pain.

The ephemeral state of love
made up by patterns of neurons
and neurotransmitters in the brain
controlled by infinite stasis and changes
in internal milieu.
It is not to hold your hand.
The trigger is somewhere in the young
for procreation and after menopause,
a difficult carrying of loneliness.
There is a difference in the aging of these.
Do we explain the state by cultures

or express by statements
of opera, books, music, and dance,
the internal feelings of love,
the opposite of loneliness.

Five thousands miles of ocean at my feet.
That is incomprehensible.
There is more that may be felt with hand or mind,
creatures reaching along the liquid
touching the sand, which is reality.

This is where it starts.
Which way is love going?
I cannot leave it behind.
There is nothing that will reach into the future.
I can give from my life nothing in the forward time.
It is so tenuous in taking into the future.
Where are the old straits?
A few tremulous trivial words to reach back
and sometime into the future and the gamble of times
and times that gamble
and care only for blood and flesh
from the great galaxies around us.
Can we find love and life there together
and every day for what reason
and pain, with Charon roaring across the river Styx

I missed you yesterday.
When did you miss me?
It is all slipping up and down in the dark hole,
the wormhole,

to the wiggly strings that are and might be.
They are not there
or they are once there
or they will be there again.
The stars move and flow in big bang
and do not come or go to the land of universes
smashing against nothing, but pure light,
which has no gravity.
Am I with or without time?
How does one turn
quickly enough to know
that this is the right direction
or is there a right direction
in this confused universe?
You are the one that I am lit for,
a calmness of demeanor
that is soothing toward a pleasure.
There is much easing,
it does not swirl needs,
and you add to this.
A woman's voice
carries all the pleasures
and a music that men do not have.
Moments with movements of the hand
that catch the breath like static,
the masculine appendages do not have.
Men lumber though life
backing into furniture
and knocking down the lamps.
It is like having a poorly mannered chimpanzee.

A woman glides and slides through the room
putting objects in proper aesthetic relationship.

There is in the kiss
the unique form of contact.
It is the last touch of a soldier to his love,
as he boards a train in 1917.
His lips were blown into shreds
by a German potato masher grenade.
There is a kiss of the daughter,
as her mother slowly dies,
to hold life together a little longer.
The kiss that lies
and the kiss
that swears eternal truth and marriage
and the kiss on a pope's ring,
a small token that bespeaks the world.

You must struggle with the rain.
You must feel the cold.
You must push the pain away.
You must feel the goal of love.
You must try day,
after day,
after day.
You must beg for the joy of love.
You must touch me.
You must be touched by men.
You must find the joy.
You will find my secrets.
Tell me your secrets.

You must know bad and good.
You must make your body
an area of warmth
or I am only feeling
the cold and space
that will never end.
Time is unfair
because I have no way to hold it.
On the edge of life
the lion roars louder than the gale.
House of anger and desire,
it is the end of the beginning.

Time has not pity.
Neither prayer
nor hope stops time.
There is no love in time.
This is our universe
without any way to open the door to a better world
that finds changes that do not bite
and asks for all the neuron cells
and endorphins of your brain.
The juices of your body
it takes loving touch without reason.
Pity, pity, pity of the universe.
The brain rots
And only flows
Of chance and struggle.

Does she wish to tell me
if I brightened her steps

and added
to the brightly colored flowers around us?
Are there unleashed fragrances
that wind from she to me
and even from me to her?
To place my hand on her arm
and feel the smooth, soft skin.
Does this touch
travel to the endorphins of the brain,
moving the synapses, hers and mine?
Can I lift spirits
and meet only scorn?
Curl the lip and shaking head
to find defeat on this day?
To carry in the breasts again,
sour and covered with scum.
I can hope and move through the day
toward the love to balance the hopes.
To ask only to accept my love.
It is a fragile gossamer brightly colored thing.
I have fashioned it from the hours
to the being me
the best I will ever be.

You must find the joy.
You find my secrets.
You must be and follow.
You must make your body
an area of warmth
for I am only feeling the cold
and space may ever end.

Hold the strength of the infinite
for I am weary of the conflict
and cannot
rise up
again,
again,
and yet
again,
so many,
many times.

Love sliding through to my being
and telling lies or truths of lies.
Where was I when she died?
She took so long to die,
cold, cold, cold,
tears, tears, tears,
end, end, end.

ANYWHERE

BY CHENELLE MCCARTNEY, AGE 14

As I sit in this car,
I think he's taking me somewhere really far.

We are going fast,
faster than a spaceship going into blast.

The seats are leather and it's smooth as a feather.

Now it's a red light and we stop.

Then all of the sudden I see rain start to drop.

The car smells like a flower,
which reminds me of baby powder.

He looks over at me and he smiles
so bright the rain stops falling.

But I think he's fake,
like a pimp trying to stop balling.

He's not telling me where we are going and I am scared
because this is worse than getting dared.
Dared to love someone that makes you cry.

It feels like your heart dies.

Then he says,
"Oops, I forgot I have to let you off here because
I never meant to take you anywhere."

REASON INDEPENDENCE

BY SIKIRA CROCKETT

Dear John,

John, sometimes people come into your life for a reason. Most people don't understand that; they just think the other person is there to fulfill their sexual or financial needs or maybe to assure them that they are the one for them—when they are really nuts.

When you are in a relationship that is moving too fast, you are not giving yourself a chance to get to know that person. It's just like being there for the moment but your mind is somewhere else. As time goes by both parties still don't know each other, so they begin to say sarcastic things to each other, things that can hurt both parties' feelings, but the stronger party doesn't understand. The weak one does. Sometimes these words are damaging to the weak party; it draws them away. They no longer want to be bothered. So the weak party is too weak for the mind, body, and soul to be hurt. So it shuts down and refuses to let anybody in again and starts to become very independent to its own needs and fulfills them all without anybody—just them.

The weak party begins to turn from weak to strong, building confidence and bringing a very high self-esteem into the party's life. But the party has now built too much pride and gratitude to still let anybody into their heart. So the party continues to accomplish their goals. Still, with independence on its side, the party can't do wrong but to keep life manageable and ask God for strength, faith, and wisdom. And now the party only needs to love themselves before they can love anybody else.

TRAIN

BY ALLEN RAYMON

While I was waiting I thought of the last time we were together. We were at this same Philadelphia railroad station standing on line to show our ticket while getting on the down escalator. Even in that public environment we managed to hiss at each other.

Going down the escalator you went backwards so that you could face me with the continuing of our argument. What was this argument about? Who remembers? There were so many back-to-back arguments that I wonder how we were able to live together for the good part of the year.

What I do remember are the initial times you asked how I would feel if you raised an objection. How did we graduate to yelling, screaming, doors slammed? Friends noticed our tenseness when we arrived at parties. By the end of the evening, we could barely contain ourselves with dirty looks at each other.

Now here I was at Amtrak waiting for the train announcement, hoping you would come running across the terminal into my arms with the two of us babbling forgiveness at the same time. The line to the down escalator started. I looked for you. Even if I saw you at the other end, there would be time for our teary get-together. As the line moved, so did my body tense.

Even on the platform, I waited. I hoped. The train pulled in and boarding was immediate. Even when the door of the train closed, I still hoped. I stayed at the door—for I couldn't move.

MARRIAGE

BY RUBY CARRASQUILLO

Here we are in the middle of nowhere. Lost as hell. She's looking at me and I'm looking at her. We just driving deeper and deeper into the woods.

Nightfall is starting to invite itself into our journey. Now she's looking at me with a wide-eyed scared-to-death look. I tell her don't worry we will be all right. I will make sure you are all right. I'll take care of you.

As we keep on going I start talking to her to relax her. I remind her of all the things that has happened to us. Like the time I was making love to her and fell asleep between her legs. And she just let me sleep. Boy did she laugh and we shared a couple of hours laughing and talking.

Then I turn on the radio, a tender song comes on. I put my hand on the seat so she can move in closer to me. So she does. I can smell her tempting perfume. As my arm hangs around her shoulder I can feel the softness of her skin as I run my fingertips up and down her arm. Her hair softly brushes across my face whenever the wind blows in my direction. She looks at me with her soft eyes. I look at her. I tell her I love you, will you marry me.

NO ORDINARY LOVE

BY ANTONIA MALDONADO

No ordinary love, you brought me T/C.

No ordinary love, we have for each other, T/C.

No ordinary love, no ordinary love.

No ordinary love, it goes on year after year, no ordinary love.

No ordinary love, what we have is so precious.

No ordinary love, what will do without each other? No ordinary love.

No ordinary love, I can't go to someone else ever. Though the men try to interest me. I will remain forever yours, no ordinary love.

No ordinary love, we speak and time melts away. Was it an hour or a few minutes, I lose time when I'm with you.

No ordinary love, the kiss of life you gave me and it remains on my lips long after you're gone. The kiss of life, no ordinary love.

No ordinary love, the pearls of wisdom you offer me and I

understand what is meant by freedom of movement, being creative and expressing myself through art and my writing, no ordinary love.

No ordinary love, no ordinary love.

No ordinary love, no ordinary love, I'll cherish the day I met you. I always will.

No ordinary love, no ordinary love.

No ordinary love, no ordinary love.

No ordinary love, no ordinary love, T/C. The earth moves, the sun shines, the rain falls down on the sidewalk. No ordinary love, no ordinary love, no ordinary love.

No ordinary love, no ordinary love.

Peaceful times in New York happen quite often in my apartment. The smells of food cooking from our corner restaurant. It permeates the air, and I think of you and cooking dinners for you.

No ordinary love, no ordinary love.

Living in a building, right here in Chelsea, fills me with joy, no other address has made me so happy. Knowing you are a part of me. No ordinary love, no ordinary love.

No ordinary love, no ordinary love. You make my life so real, other neighbors come and go but I feel your presence all of the time.

No ordinary love, no ordinary love.

No ordinary love, no ordinary love. I eat my breakfast of wheat bread, coffee and soon you will be knocking on my door very loud and very familiar. No ordinary love, no ordinary love, no ordinary love.

No ordinary love, no ordinary love, cooking meatloaf with onions, garlic, cilantro, salt and pepper and thyme. Adding hard boiled eggs into the meatloaf. Serving baby carrots, beef gravy to go over Uncle Ben's rice and tortillas. Corona Extra beer to go along with everything.

No ordinary love, no ordinary love. We go to Irish pubs for the best hamburgers with bacon, cheese and onions and French fries and lettuce and tomatoes. You have a Corona Extra and I have a Diet Coke.

I love going to Mexican restaurants and we always order Chicken Poblano with refried beans and great rice with lettuce and tomatoes. You have Corona Extra and I have Diet Coke.

Dessert is flan and coffee and most important there is always music. No ordinary love, no ordinary love.

No ordinary love, no ordinary love. I bought you Octavio Paz's works, Edgar Allen Poe and so many others like Stephen King, and you gave me J.R.R. Tolkien. The Dark Tower with the gunslinger. You refused to mail a card saying I didn't want the complete works of Hemingway, which I am grateful for.

No ordinary love, no ordinary love.

No ordinary love, no ordinary love.

No ordinary love, no ordinary love. I found the theme song of *Phantom of the Opera* in my CD cabinet and knew you had placed it there for me.

No ordinary love, no ordinary love.

GOD TENSED IN AN AIRLINE SEAT

GOD

BY GERRY BOGACZ

God burst in
Through the windows
Nestled in the minds
Of His faithful
Whose lips whispered
Pious pleas
As their hands
Wrought anger
From the sky

God sought out
The unbelieving
Through the actions
Of His servants
Unleashing hatred
For salvation
Promises of paradise
After death
After carnage

God tensed in
An airline seat
Amid frantic thoughts
A heart racing
Prayers and pleadings
In final minutes
Asking that

The cup might pass
A victim nonetheless
God stood trapped
In heat and smoke
As other victims
Invoked His names
And leapt into
Vast emptiness
As a desperate choice
Between burning
Or a final fall

God was on
The winding stairs
In panicked minds
Of those who fled
And thought of others
Amid their escape
And climbed
With those
Who offered help

God was
What humans
Made of Him
On a gruesome day
Bent to
Their purposes
And needs
Soldier
Solace
He was all of us

THE SECRET

BY MYRA K. BAUM

Wish upon a star.

So many wishes
How do you choose?
Which to grant
Which to deny

Let the secret out

Do you rate them,
or grade them?

Are so many granted
For dogs
From boys and girls under ten
For mates
From those over 40?

Tell us
Are there right wishes
Wrong wishes

Let the secret out.

WHY IS LIFE THE WAY IT IS?

BY CHENELLE MCCARTNEY, AGE 14

Why is life the way it is?
It's harder than a math quiz.
Why are so many things so wrong?
Like rappers getting killed over a song.
Why did God make us the way we are?
Like when we fall we get a scar.
Why was the love made?
It's sadder than losing a game at the arcade.
Or more hurtful than to get stepped on at a parade.
Why do people make each other sad?
So sad, it's not being mad.
Why do people kill each other?
Worse than watching your mom have
your newborn brother.
That's why I don't understand the way life is!!!

SOUND

BY LESLIE BROWN

When I hear you ringing in my ear
That melancholic sound makes me want to tear

I listen tentatively to your voice
Sometimes I feel like I want to rejoice

Your melody sends me into a slumber
After a while my mind often wonders

Is this sound I'm hearing an angel
Or is this sound some sort of jungle

I wonder these things because it sounds so sweet
I just can't help but stomp my feet

I pat my hands, I try to sing along
If only I knew all the words to your song

It gives me great vibes just to listen
If I were a piece of crystal glass…I'd probably glisten

That's why I have to have you close and near
That's right nice and close to my ear

I close this moment remembering your sweet sound
Thinking at all times how it has me bound

CALLING THE CHILDREN: SEPTEMBER 11, 2004

BY LISA FENGER

That morning, after a moment of silence, the calling for the children began. Into the morning air, one by one for hours, mothers and fathers stood where their children had vanished and called for them by name. They called into the sky and down into the pit, they searched the heavens, their hearts, the depths of the dust of the earth, and not finding them, they cast flowers onto the silent pools in their despair. Where do dead children live?

On that day, and daily, I stand with them in grief. My own children are missing. They are not in the heavens, the earth, the depths of my body. They are only in my heart, they are nameless; I cannot conceive of them. Where shall I search? I have no flowers still fragile with life to place in the pools of my memory. Where do unborn children live?

When the outward calling for the children was complete, I staggered upwards to the surface and into the sanctuary of a church. There the priest told of the horror when the slaughter of children began. In his hand, he held oil born of the olives of Spain where also the murder of children took place. "Come" he said, and lines formed silently to be anointed.

In a time beyond time I stood, my hands in his, my eyes in his, my soul vanished in the pit. "What do you desire?" he asked.

"To be okay," I answered, having no name for the vast unfathomable emptiness swirling around me and in me and through me, the mother who did not mother me, the father who did not protect me, the children dead in this place, the parents who cry for them, the mother I will never be, the children wasting inside me, the child I was wasted at the hands of my parents, the wrongness so terrible that there is no name, only a prayer that it be made right. "I want to be okay."

Gently, he asked my name, the name that teachers have torn from me, the name my parents do not say in my presence or absence, the name praying for the return of its soul so that all will be made well.

"Lord," the priest whispered for only my ears and God's, "here is Lisa, your daughter," and through the silence and time, across the pit and the air of the heavens and the dust of the earth, past the fading of flowers and unfilled pools, to wherever lost souls live, I heard the cry and the call: "Lisa, my child, where are you?" And I lifted my head and was marked with oil and was found.

LIKE HORSES

BY JANA LINDAN-IHRIE

Like horses we will not be saved.

We rear up, wrench free
And run back to the barn
Into the flames.

Oh, we shriek,
And keen
And worry each new wound

But when the flames again leap high,
Like horses
we will not be saved.

We refuse to be led
Into the
Dark unknown.

Like horses
Back to the flames
We go

The only home
We know.

AUTUMN GRAVES

BY MYLES GIBBONS

Desiccated and despairing days,
widow-weeded and pensioned;
nights beneath a waxed and yellowed moon.

Descend from fevered dreams;
unwind the surgeon's swaddling,
and follow.

We'll float down fog-green, ghosted streets,
damp-cobbled lanes, as slippery as redemption,
while autumn graves gape with toothless maws.

TULIPS, PANTYHOSE, AND MORE

TULIPS

BY MYRA K. BAUM

One tulip
Personifying
A new season.
Flowers on city blocks
Spring saturating our sight.

Tulips and smiles
Elegance, simplicity
Designed by nature
Color, freshness
In one perfect form

Evoke
Signs of springs past
Sleeveless dresses
In 50's fabric
Upfront in East Village shops

Displayed with matching
Spring coats and toppers
Crinolines and club jackets
Anticipating
Purchases
By those born after the Fifties.

PANTYHOSE

BY JUDY TAYLOR

Netlike, surrounded with netting
Suffocating, entangling my body
Restrained mercilessly
A second skin encircling me!
A reticulating boa constrictor of a snake
That's pantyhose!

1,2,3,4,3,2,1

BY SHUNN THEINGI, AGE 9

Big
Hippo Giant
Drinking Eating Sleeping
Mouse is very small
Hiding Running Moaning
Mouse Rat Small

A LIST

BY GABRIELLE REM

blooming flowers
green grass
galloping horses
cherry blossom trees
calm waters
seasons changing
kids playing
people rollerblading
runners, joggers, walkers
horseback riders
squirrels scurrying
birds chirping
hawks preying
pigeons cooing (shitting)
dogs barking
breezes swooshing
trees swaying
rats rustling
leaves falling
colors turning
serenity
tranquility
amidst the chaotic jungle of cement

TIRE ROLLING DOWN THE STREET

BY LEATRICE JENKINS

The first thing that comes to my mind about a tire rolling down the street is the Rolling Stones. I'm quite sure that they have made most of their music on the road. Getting the beat out of hearing the tires on the highways and byways, as they went to their next gig. Sometimes I bet that in their sleep they feel the rhythm and moments of sound of the calling trees giving way to the success of another hit record.

Hey, maybe it's a relaxing way for them to come down off of the excitement and joy of performing in front of millions and millions of people all over the world. But hey, who knows, this is my tire rolling down the street. Maybe the Rolling Stones never made a hit to rolling tires.

MY HEAD IS SWEATING...

BY ANDREW LEONG, AGE 6

My head is sweating.
It is very hot.
The sun is yellow.
I saw something, a purple square.
The weather is very hot in my head.
I saw something white
I saw a white circle. The sun is going to blow up.
The sun is very, very super hot.
The sun is going to blow up like a volcano.

I HAVE A SECRET ABOUT MY EYE

BY LINDA SOLLITTO

I have a secret that I never told anybody. I have only a glass eye and no one can tell. When I go to sleep I take it out and wash it and put it in a little cup I have in my drawer that I lock. In the morning I get up early so no one sees that it's out. I take a shower and I put it back in like it was never out. And nobody knew it was out.

P.S. I like to talk to my eye and sometimes I play marbles with it.

FUDGE!

BY TERRY NORTON

In my house, Great Grandma's Fudge has been the hallmark of the Christmas season. Take your millions of lights and moving Santa lawns and lines of shoppers the day after Thanksgiving. We knew Christmas had truly arrived when Mom pulled out her huge iron pot and put in four ounces of shaven unsweetened chocolate, two cups of sugar and one cup of milk and began to bring it to a slow rolling boil.

By this time of year in Connecticut, it was cold and snow covered the ground. We were driven inside to suffer through endless weekend football games. Then the sweet smell of the confection would reach us in the living room and pull us to the source. The smell of Christmas was calling. Mom would gently stir the bubbling concoction and every once in a while, drip some into a cup of cold water. She would twirl the glass and poke the brown mass in the bottom. I never knew what she was looking for—some magic moment that I was not yet privy to. After what seemed an eternity of stirring, dripping and sloshing, she would announce, "It's ready. Get the plate."

The plate, the special plate used only for cooling the Fudge. It is a huge moritaki platter that traveled from Japan and back twice, once to Germany and all over the country during Dad's military career. The Fudge plate, sacred and honored for its role in this holy holiday. Ever so carefully, Mom would pour the thick chocolate goo from arm's height to the pot then over a wooden spoon onto the plate. It spread out slowly in a shiny smooth circle.

Now we waited. Mom would poke the substance in the plate several times before calling, "It's ready." She poured a teaspoon of vanilla extract on top of the soft shell of chocolate. The Fudge now became a family project. With a wooden spoon, we each took turns stirring the mass to mix in air and bring it to a dry but malleable consistency. Soon, Dad would have to hold the plate while the stirrer used both hands and all his or her body weight to move it through the thickening mass. All during the process, the trick was to get some of the fudge on your hand or finger so you had to lick it off. That was very important, because you were not allowed to put your hands anywhere near your mouth for the next step.

Sleeves up, hands shining clean we dug into the dough and began kneading and molding it. Mom would lay out rolls of wax paper as we worked the clay to form logs. Sometimes, the moisture in your hands would turn it all back into a liquidy mess. That meant it had not cooked long enough, and we had to start over.

Each log was rolled about 1" in diameter and 6" long. We laid them on the wax paper, and Mom rolled them up. The first log she would always cut up and lay out. When all the Fudge was made, there would be the succulent tidbits waiting for us to wrap our taste buds around. Ambrosia. We sighed as the rich confectionary began melting in our mouths. Christmas had truly arrived.

These days, Mom doesn't make the Fudge. She has arthritis and no one to stir it or hold the plate when it gets thick. I am the official Fudge maker. I learned what magic sign Mom looked for that told her the Fudge was ready. My son can hold the plate while I stir, and we can switch. I cut up the first log, I roll them in the wax paper. I then wrap them in tin foil, wrapping paper, mailing paper and send them to my brothers' families. Christmas has arrived, when Great Grandma's Fudge is on the table.

Time to put up the tree.

I KNEW IT WAS MY MOTHER

BY NAJIER MATTHEWS, AGE 14

My mother has this look to her.
She's light skinned.
She's not really fat,
but she has some weight on her.
She's not one of those skinny women,
but she is shaped like a professional model.

Thick.

She has this walk to her
when she comes up the block.
It's like she tries to look good,
but she does not switch a lot like those "chicken heads!"

If she has on a dress, it sways back and forth as she moves.
She has a good taste in clothes,
not too dark and definitely not too light.

Her favorite word is Damn!
Everything is Damn!
"Why didn't you finish your 'damn' homework?"

If you get her mad she will curse you out.
She be "keeping it real."

SEX 1

BY ESTHER TORRES

One day my son saw two dogs having sex, so one dog was looking east and the other dog was looking west. So he told me, Mommy, Mommy, look, someone tied the two dogs together, please, Mommy, untie them please. He was crying and he was nine years old. And he saw sex at the age of nine but did not know what it was.

SEX 2

BY ESTHER TORRES

Sex is love and tenderness
Sex is bad and good
Sex is caring and hugging
Sex is a fool that cries
Sex has many things with it.

I SEE A BARBARIAN...

BY MICHELLE LEI, AGE 9

I see a barbarian
I hope he's American

Some things are outrageous
That could be contagious

Cool things are wizards
Cold things are blizzards

When you see the sunrise
It is quite a surprise

THREE HAIKU

BY SYD LAZARUS

Summer sun burns my skin
though I don't feel it yet—
Later comes the pain.

A summer fruit the lovely peach
waiting for my touch and bite.
I reach for it.

The cat stares—
Does she see anything?—
then jumps off the couch.

POEM

BY ANGELICA MERCHAN, AGE 7

Go
Red, green
Going, stopping, slowing
I am going home
Stop

POEM

BY TIFANY MERCHAN, AGE 9

Pencils
Very sharp
Writing, sharpening, scraping
Using words on paper
Writing

MORNING MOMENT

BY KATY MORGAN

(Verse)

I cannot tell how long ago it was.
A week or two? Not long, and yet I feel
It's been too long. Yes, I will go again!
The pastry shop across the street is there,
Day in, day out, and always tempting me.
I enter. Yes, the girl remembers me,
And reaches even as I ask for it
To put a golden pastry in the bag,
I love their croissants, and the almond rolls
Are heavenly, but only the brioches
Are perfect, and the sales clerk knows
What I will ask for every time I come.
The money changes hands and I look up
To see the baker standing by the door
Behind the counter, watching what I buy.
He's new; I never saw this one before.
Can he bake as well the perfect cakes
And cookies too, and can the pastries he
Bakes be as good as those I know and love?
Outside again, I open up the bag
And sniff, and take a careful tiny bite:
It tastes as good as I remember it,
The odor fills my nostrils, yes it is
As heavenly as ever. Ah, what joy!

I eat a bit, then put the rest away,
To get my card out, pay my fare, go in,
Walk up the platform to the perfect place
For getting out again at Fourteenth Street.
Why don't I walk today? I ask myself.
The weather's perfect, and it's not too far.
It costs a dollar, taking train and bus,
And takes almost as long as walking there.
Yes, but, it only costs a dollar and
Old habits die hard. Try another time.

(Prose)

So, I thought, well, in case I get hungry, and I haven't had one of those wonderful brioches in a while, well, so what if I already had a doughnut this morning, so I left a few minutes early and went across the street to get a brioche at Patisserie Claude. There was a new baker in the back, I saw, so when I opened up the bag on my way down the street I bit into the brioche suspiciously: is it different? Well, I couldn't tell any difference, it was delicious, so I'm eating it as I go in the subway to take the number one to Fourteenth Street. I'm thinking, how long has it been since I walked the mile and a half over to the Y, and today, with this weather, there's no excuse, it takes just as long to take the subway and bus, and it costs a dollar, but then it only costs a dollar...

POEM

BY MICHELLE LEI, AGE 9

Black Book   Black Blue
Black Bee   Black Bazooka
Black Bomb   Black Boots
Black Bat   Black Baboon
Black Beach   Black Bird
Black Braces   Black Butter
Black Bubble   Black Band
Black Boar   Black Board

BLUE

BY YVONNE FOLK

I am feeling blue today
My father has a blue car
I have two blue coats
I have a blue bag
That hat is blue
I have two pair of blue shoes
My door is blue
Yvonne is blue today
I have three dresses and they are blue

DEAD RAT HAMBURGERS

DEAD RAT HAMBURGERS

BY TIFFANY WONG, AGE 8

Materials

1. 18 dead rats
2. 2 hairy tomatoes
3. Bleu cheese
4. Moldy bread
5. Blood (optional: shoot a person with a bazooka gun to get the blood.)
6. Grater
7. Bowl
8. Spoon
9. Hair

Steps

1. Grate bleu cheese and drop 3 gallons of blood into the bowl
2. Dice tomato
3. Wash dead mice or rat in blood*
4. Cook rats
5. Put everything together

Stink up and enjoy!

*Do not dry

PANTOUM

BY SYD LAZARUS

Two subjects I don't do well in:
Poetry and math—
A long twenty-five minutes.
Forget about Pantoums

Poetry and math:
Add, subtract, multiply, divide—
Forget about Pantoums.
Write about the day.

Add, subtract, multiply, divide,
We were taught in school.
Write about the day
We learned about Pantoums.

We were taught in school
English, history, French, algebra,
We learned about Pantoums.
I was a bad student of poetry.

English, history, French, algebra,
Poetry and math.
I was a bad student of poetry—
A long twenty-five minutes.

EYES

BY EDDIE LAWSON, AGE 10

Eyes
Everyone has them.

You use them to see different things.

Everywhere you go you see
Something different.
Someone please help me find my
Homework.

JUMP TO THE MOON

BY CLAUDIA RACIBORKSI, AGE 7

Jump to the Moon

1. Get 2 plates
2. Put 7 red evil pizzas
3. Get 1 live walking band
4. Add blood to it
5. Save it for 1 day

Give it to anyone.

When somebody eats it, they will jump to the moon.

WALKING SHOES

BY HARRY M. MAHN

I dropped a CD into the player, turned out the lights and crawled into bed. Just as I was sliding into slumber with melodies of Peruvian flute music floating by, I heard the door creak and saw light shoot in from the outside hall. I bolted upright in the bed. There, at the door, I saw my loafers shuffling out into the hall entirely by themselves. It was really weird.

The door closed behind them and I was again left in darkness. But somehow—and I can't explain this—I was able to watch the progress of my loafers as they made their way to the elevators. They stopped and patiently waited. In a few moments, the elevator doors opened to let off a pizza delivery person. Before the doors could close again, the loafers hopped on.

Upon reaching the lobby, the loafers got out. They shuffled past the concierge and out the front door that was being kept open by a doorman watching girls and enjoying the balmy summer weather.

The loafers paused, turned right, and shuffled up the avenue. Where, I wondered, were these loafers off to? Two blocks away, they stopped at an Irish pub. I was amazed. They were actually going in. Once inside, they made their way to the bar and slid under the stool of a remarkably attractive redhead with a terrific pair of legs. She was chatting with the bartender.

The bar was filling up and clusters of people began swirling around. How could my loafers take all the smoke, I wondered? I, myself, only entered bars to meet people with whom I had arranged to have something to eat. I rarely stayed in a bar. The noise and smoke put me off. Could my loafers actually find this place congenial?

The bartender had moved on to serve others. A young professional type took a stool next to the lady, and began chatting with her. They seemed to get along well—what with them shaking with laughter, and, occasionally, spilling some of their drinks. I couldn't believe seeing one of my loafers actually hop sideways to catch a bit of splashed booze in his heel.

A wing-tipped shoe on the young man's foot looked down and said to my loafer, "Hey, you down there, you really like the hooch."

"My goodness, Mr. Wingtip actually talks. Who would have thought?" my slightly tipsy loafer replied.

"Hey, wise-ass, I was just trying to make conversation. If I weren't tied to this yuppie's foot, I'd break your insoles."

"Touchy, touchy," replied my loafer. "Actually, I'm glad you spoke. I was getting bored. Do you spend a lot of time here?"

"Not that much. My guy's a lawyer. Works around the clock. With the kind of schedule he keeps, I'll be getting bagged and tossed down the chute in a couple of months. Him socializing with a babe, like the one you're under, is about as good as it gets for me. But, say, how did you manage to free yourself? Did your guy pass out?"

My loafers rocked with laughter. "Pass out? My guy's practically a teetotaler."

"So, how did you do it?" asked the wingtips.

"It's really very strange," said my loafer. "I was assembled in a Georgia factory by Pedro, an illegal Peruvian with false papers. After his shift, Pedro'd usually relax by having a few beers, puffing a joint, and playing on his wind pipes. After only two months on the job, he, along with everybody else, got notice that the factory was being closed. The company could no longer compete with shoes from China.

"I was the last pair Pedro would be working on, and he decided to vent by putting a spell on me. He rubbed on some of his spit, said some hocus pocus, and then hummed tunes from the place where he was born. When he was finished with me, he began laughing and walked out of the factory.

"I hadn't the slightest idea as to what Pedro had done. The conveyor took me to the end of the line, and there I was boxed and shipped like all the other loafers. Then, one night, as the guy who bought me gets ready to go to bed, he puts on a CD with Peruvian music. Slowly, I begin getting hot all over and find myself starting to shuffle. Anyway, here I am."

"Hey, man, I never heard that one before . . . unbelievable," said the wingtip.

"Yeah, I can't believe it either," replied my loafer. "Anyway, I and my left shoe, here, have got to go. The smoke's getting too heavy."

My loafers then slipped out from under the redhead's stool and shuffled out of the bar. They seemed less steady than when they left the apartment earlier that evening.

I went to my door and looked down the hallway to the elevators. The doors opened and the loafers hopped off. As they shuffled towards me, I could see that they looked truly worn and tired. They were taking their place under my bed, when I let them know in no uncertain terms that there would be no more Peruvian flute music, and that, in the morning, they would be getting a good polishing.

I WISH I HAD A METAL CHEST...

BY ANDREW LEONG, AGE 6

I wish I had a metal chest.
I wish I had a gold head.
I wish I had a body that could open and I had a lot
    of stuff in it
I wish I could fly by flying on my head.
I wish I had fire hands.
I wish I could make a spirit bomb and I was 10 years old.
I wish I had a special lab and car.
I wish I had laser eyes.
I wish I had long feet that are invisible.
I wish I had 100 brains and there were specks all over
    my head.
I wish I could turn invisible.
I wish I could fly with my feet because there are Martians
    all over my legs
and they go to my feet.
I wish I had attacks like fire breath, laser vision, lightning
    control,
power lightning fingers, and magic stretching feet.
I wish I had hair that is very sharp.
I wish I had claws.

WHEN I WAS LITTLE...

BY BRIAN LEONG, AGE 5

When I was little I peed in my pants.
Today I went to a trip at school and saw dinosaur bones.

GO UPWARDS OR BE THROWN DOWN

ELEVEN IS A HARD PLACE TO STAND

BY JUDIE DAVID

I could see the yard over their heads.
A superior smirk was my greeting to those eight-year-olds.
I had to be careful to always be above them,
not of them.
The fourteen-year-olds rushed the yard.
I could see only as high as their neckties.

My parents gave me a world and I saw it through their
        frame.
It was a liberal, non-observant Jewish world.
My world.

My world was shattered from within
by my mother's pain: head pounding muffled by tight
        bandana,
the room dark as a morgue.
A rope cordoned us off from the rest of the austere world.
My father was the light that pierced all of it,
helping old ladies with their shopping,
and delighting in Mozart, and I could see to the other
        side.

My best friend, Susie, and I played apartment-house
        handball.
On the catch we talked "when I grow up."

I wanted to be a ballet dancer until I found that I
    couldn't.
Susie wanted only what was most unlikely;
a movie star or a gymnast.

I sped around ice rinks and jeté-d across stages
trying to black out my mother's suffering.
The faster I went around rinks,
the higher my "Stop" sign went against growing up,
even though I knew at eleven
I had to go upwards or be thrown down.

WHEN I'M 25

BY LYNETTE MORREN, AGE 14

When I be 25, I won't be a hoe.

I won't be broke.

I won't have more than three kids.

I won't be with a man that don't love me
 or don't like to work.

I won't be working at a cheap job.

If my 25-year-old self could see me now,
she would be like:
Oh, my God, look at you—
so surprised.

DECISIONS OF FIGHT OR FLIGHT

BY ELAINE DRAYTON

Growing up in the Sixties was not easy. It was a time when a person had to make decisions of fight or flight. My mother was a strict disciplinarian, and one of her rules was "no fighting among ourselves or with others." She used to say that "a good run is better than a bad stand and Jesus turned the other cheek, so you kids take a lesson from that." She didn't know that I had a conversation with one of the brothers from the hall and he said, "Do what you have to do because even Jesus ran out of cheeks." Then there were the times when she would say, "Don't be a bully. Don't stand fights. Bullies are really cowards. If you have to defend yourself, pick up anything at hand, give them your best, knock them out, and run home to me. No one is going to touch you. God and I will take it from there." I kept all these things in mind and pondered over them from time to time.

I attended Cooper Junior High School, located on 119th Street between Madison Avenue and Fifth Avenue. It was not easy going to school there because there was a group of girls at Cooper who picked on everybody and kicked ass just because they felt like it. I happened to be one of the ones they loved to pick on. I knew it was because I wouldn't fight back. I didn't fight back because my mother wouldn't like it and I was afraid of what she would do when she found out.

Yet it was getting harder and harder not to fight. I was not afraid of them. They were just making me angrier and angrier, and it was hard to concentrate in class. To say the least, it was most embarrassing.

Anyway, this particular day Ruby and Andrea decided that I would be the whipping post for the day. They started by tripping me up in the hall and throwing dirt on my blouse on the playground. Ruby and Andrea loved to fight, they even had boys afraid of them. They and their friends wreaked chaos through the neighborhood. I for one was really sick and tired of them. They had my back up against the wall. They said, "What you gonna do about it, ha ha? What ya gonna do?"

Well, before I could think I blurted out, "I'll fight you. I'll fight you after school. I'll meet you outside."

They released me and said, "See ya, hate to be ya. Don't be late." They walked away laughing and slapping each other five.

While sitting in class, I couldn't think. My mind was on the fight I had coming up and I was wishing I could reach back in time and shut my mouth. I wanted so bad to take back those words. I did not see this happening. I saw my cousin Terry and I told her that I was going to have a fight with Ruby or Andrea. She said, "I'll be there. I'll make sure it's a fair fight." She was a grade ahead of me, but we shared the same gym. I knew she would watch my back.

As the day progressed, I kept wishing I could change my mind. As the time approached for school to let out and I became more nervous and anxious as the hour of doom galloped upon me, I was a wreck with indecision. The thought of running through the back door had crossed my mind several times throughout the day. Yet I couldn't turn tail and run. I refused to be that kind of coward. My word was my bond, and I couldn't take it back, come hell or high water. I feared getting into more trouble for not keeping my word than for fighting. Mom was more adamant about a person keeping their word. I could hear her in my head saying, "Your word is all you get that's yours. It makes you who you are. It's the only thing you have that's worth anything."

Getting my ass kicked by Ruby or Andrea was not in my plans. I had to come out on top, since I more than likely would get my behind torn up by Mom when she found out. And find out she would, because bad news seems to travel on the wind, especially the news you don't want known. Word had gotten around school that I would be fighting Ruby or Andrea. Now I definitely couldn't change my mind. At three o'clock the bell rang, the hour I was dreading had arrived. It was time to piss in the pot.

As I approached the doors, I could hear the crowd outside waiting. Their sound was roaring in my ears, along with the beating of my heart. I could hear the kids screaming, "There's going to be a fight. Elaine is fighting Ruby. No, she's fighting Andrea." I was all up in my head talking to myself, saying, "I don't want to be here. I don't want to go through those doors." I wished I could click my heels three times and find myself home, but that wasn't happening, either.

The decision of whether to go through those doors was taken out of my hands, because the kids behind and around me who were screaming and waiting for something to happen opened the door and they sort of push-carried me outside.

The park was right across the street, and the other kids kept pushing and shoving me to the park. When I got there, everyone moved back, giving us room to face each other. My cousin was right there in the crowd saying, "You better whip her ass."

Well, I could feel the hair on the back of my neck standing on end. I could taste my sweat. I wished I could close my eyes and upon opening them, find myself someplace else.

However, in for a penny, in for a pound, I was here for the whole round. Standing before each other sweating and hearts beating fast, we were shouting and gesturing at one another to throw the first lick. "Hit me. Hit me. No, you hit me, I dare ya!" We kept going back and forth with this for a bit, but the crowd had not come to hear this. They came to see action. Someone in the crowd pushed her into me and me into her. As we came together, we were kicking and scratching and pulling hair. We were fighting like wildcats; nothing and no one could stop us. The only thing that stopped the fight was the sound of sirens, police sirens. Once we heard them, we got into the wind like a flock of pigeons taking flight. We scattered in every direction. No one wanted to be taken home by the police.

Even though I had a hard time as a teen with fighting, it seems sweet now, compared to the back-stabbing and shooting that the teens engage in nowadays.

The next day when I came to school, the girls pulled me into their circle. Andrea came up to me throwing her arms around my shoulders, pulling and holding me to her like I was a long lost friend or something. She said, "You gonna hang with us." She had her arms around me, hugging me, and I couldn't say no. She was nodding to her girls and saying, "Yeaha, yeaha. She's one of us now."

Well I was really ready to pee in my pants. No way was I about to join a gang. They might as well kill me, because I knew my mother would. I was more scared of her than anybody. Andrea and Ruby and her friends had another thing coming, cause believe me, I was not going to get caught up with their dumb asses. No way, no how. I had to get away from these fools without getting a real beat down. I decided I'd let them down slow and easy.

Next thing I know, I'm hanging with these fools, sneaking around, playing hooky from school. Getting into all kinds of things. I'm living a double life and it's not easy running around like a chicken without a head, doing dumb stuff crazy.

ORPHAN OF THE STORM
PROLOGUE: CHICAGO—WINTER 1968

BY JANA LINDAN-IHRIE

A fierce blizzard howled down out of Canada and hit the entire Chicago area. Yale Elementary closed early. Outside of the school, cars were lined up bumper to bumper up and down the block. Some of the children didn't have rides, they traveled on foot, or rode the City Buses; Melissa lived close enough to walk home.

"Go right home, children," the seventh grade teacher calls out, hurrying students down the hall. "This is a bad storm!" she warns, as they file out the door. "And no snow-ball fights."

As soon as the kids get outside they squeal and giggle, happy to be out of school early—but Melissa inwardly groans. She doesn't want to go home today at all, much less early. This is the first day of her father's off-duty time. He's always drunk on his days off. Sometimes he's gone for the first day, or even until the late night hours of the second day, but other times, he spends the entire time drinking at the kitchen table. She never knows if he'll be there, until she gets home from school.

Melissa only has five blocks to walk, but the snow is already so deep she can hardly make her way through the building drifts, and the wind is gusting with such force, she can barely see but a few feet ahead. About halfway home, a tall building partially blocks the wind, and Melissa sees a stretch of snow unbroken by a single footprint. It looks so like a big, bouncy cloud that she runs over, spins around and flops down on her back to make a snow-angel. She pumps her arms and legs back and forth just as she and her father had done when she was little.

"Come on, kids," her daddy would call. "Let's get out in the snow before it's all trampled down."

Melissa stops moving, saddened by the sure knowledge that her father no longer wants to make snow-angels, or help build a snowman with a carrot nose. And next summer, she knows he won't take her swimming in the lake either. Just thinking about how much fun they used to have makes her eyes brim and her stomach ache. She wishes she could understand why he has to drink now and be so mean. Pulling up her knees, she rolls onto her side and curls into a ball to ease the pain. She weeps—there in the snow's soft hush—until her cheeks burn and smart and snowflakes hang heavy on her lashes and then fall to melt on her up-turned face.

By the time Melissa turns back over and gets to her feet, her snow-jacket is covered stiff with heavy, wet flakes. Shivering, she swipes at her drippy nose with the inside of her sleeve. Surprised to see that the streetlamps are lit, she wonders if she had slipped off to sleep. She watches the snow swirl and sparkle in the glow from the light-poles overhead, marveling the way endless snow-flakes float like magic out of the dark sky. How she wishes she could be a snowflake and whirl away and never have to go home again. "Please, God," she murmurs aloud. "Don't let him be there."

Melissa glances down and sees her snow-angel is all but gone in the drifting snow. Just like her daddy—all but gone. She sighs, yanks her wooly hat low over her ears, ducks her head against the wind, and plods on home through the storm.

ODYSSEY

BY MYLES GIBBONS

On a dark and urban island
she rides a silvered skateboard,
long pale hair flowing in the breeze.

She's been running most of her life,
breathing hope or hopelessness.
Sweet and sad, she skates the night.

Her swan-white skin reflects the moon,
while her arms, held high, beg for
blame or blessing.

Past steamy, misty manholes she skims,
chased or chasing, she rides solitary streets.
In love with love or loneliness she slides.

For Casey

NIGHT SWEEPS

BY ANN QUINTANO

They ought to put a bed down here. So many women huddle along the cold tile floor of the Penn Station bathroom hoping for some clustered moments of sleep that it would only be merciful to have a bed. No sooner does the women's breathing shift—deeper more rhythmic, a musical accompaniment to REM sleep—than the police enter on their regular rounds to rouse and disperse the women. The bathroom matrons, as sometimes do the police, rely on Virginia—former teacher, now homeless—the self-appointed matron of the space—to help ease people out. She encourages this one, nudges that one, sweeps up disarrayed belongings of another.

But Margaret is too heavily and desperately asleep—too long deprived and disheartened. A cop, Kojak, as we call him, all massive bulk and clean-shaven head, approaches her and slams his police baton against the wall some feet above her head. It cracks loud and fierce but there are only sounds of love grumblings, hissing from her throat and lungs, and an almost imperceptible twinge of her leg. I keep one eye peeled on her and one carefully on Kojak as I slowly feign gathering my possessions in order to buy time so I can keep vigil. Kojak moves towards the other end of her body, striding with a rigid military air, and heaves a kick hard onto the sole of her right foot. She gasps and starts.

"Move it!" he yells and swings around fast toward me feeling the heat of my eyes upon him.

I dip my eyes down and heave up my bag and move edging to Margaret's side as she struggles to her feet. Kojak is moving round the room now much like a caged animal and running his bat sharply over the tile walls.

"C'mon—out all of you bitches—outta here." He falls in behind us (Margaret and me, the stragglers) pounding the wall behind us and herding us like animals to the slaughter.

"Line up against the wall," he shouts and some dozen women bedraggled and exhausted welcome the wall to help keep us standing. Mary teeters, her eyes half closed. Her thin calves poke out from her skirt like a blue heron's spindly legs. Her own legs are twitching tremendously. Kojak drives us on now marching us through hallways of lower Penn Station and up the escalator. We can feel the heavy drafts blowing in from the opened gates and doorways— another tactic used to drive the homeless out. Blasts of cold air alternating with suffocating heat. The ram, ram, ram of his bat follows us and he strides rudely and darkly behind us snickering, then letting go a barrage of ugly comments. He drives us out onto Eighth Avenue where the cold bleakness reserved for three a.m. is whipping up short, hard blasts of air and dampness. I send a quick glance to Margaret again, who is ill-protected in a short sleeve shirt, and register a further worry for her well-being. We spread out now as he blathers at us: "STAY OUT" and we roam a short distance in various directions, our legs swollen and leaden and decidedly unable to carry us any further.

After years on the street I have come to believe that one can fairly die for lack of sleep and that waking and sleeping begin to merge in some horrific limbo that is the walking night terror of people who are homeless. Not long after this incident set in the 1980s, Penn Station closed off all those areas. They redesigned a more homeless-proof bathroom and so escalated vigilance that women hardly ever find sanctuary there. Where do they find it? I worry. For everyplace and nearly everyone, it seems, continues to say: "Stay out."

WHAT MATTERS, THEN?

BY TANIA HEAD

I see your face, look in your eyes,
And I see it.
I listen to your words,
And I see it.
I look at the way you keep your hands close to you,
And I see it.

I see it everywhere, I cannot shut it down.
It happens here, in Russia, in Egypt, in Gaza.
It's ever present.
It's taking over.
It's winning, I'm losing.
I can't stop it. I don't know how.
I'm angry, I hate it.
It's in me, I want it out.
It's in the boy from Russia who I saw on TV.
I saw it.

It's here, it's there, it's everywhere.
It's in my head, it's in my skin, it's in me.
I swallowed it and it won't leave me.

I want to take it off, I want a pair of hands that can
reach deep in me and remove it.
Remove it from me, from those children, from this
earth.

Take it away, but to where?
Paradise? We can't take it there because it's there too.
Paradise is no longer a place for lovers, it's a place for martyrs.

I need to find a person who can do it.
A person who can stop it.
A person who has the power.
A person who saw it and is not blinded like I am.

It's an epidemic.
It's spreading and there's no cure.
It changes people.
It makes us weak, angry and guilty.
Once you see it, you cease to exist.

You saw it, I saw it.
Who's left?
Soon there'll be no one left.

Run, run, before it's too late.
Hide in the caves,
Shield yourself from this overtaking.
Tape, plastic, masks,
Whatever it takes.

Hide your children,
Build walls around cities that separate families.
Close borders,
Take fingerprints at airports,
Divide people by their skin color,

Look at their names and take them off planes.
Isolate yourself.

And in the end,
What matters, then?

TILL DEATH DO US PART?

BY YOLANDA SIMON

Hey, "psssp." You, yeah you. Can I talk to you for a minute?

Hey, remember me? Well I remember you very well. Anyway, let me refresh your memory. The first time we met, we spoke for a while. You were really down that day. You said you felt less than nothing and you wanted to die.

Till death do us part!

That night you took me home with you. You did all kinds of things with me. You were so vulnerable. You should have asked your friends about me. They fell in love with me. It was love at first sight.

Till death do us part!

The days and the nights that followed, we became a team. We were like Bonnie and Clyde. Wherever you were, I was right beside you. You would be up, you would be down. I mean really down. Girl, did you look so stupid at times. We would have long conversations. Talking to you can be so boring sometimes, because you would be on one subject for hours.

Till death do us part!

As time went by your world began to revolve around me. I was always there when you needed me, right? You were all mine. It was then that I knew you would do anything to keep me by your side. When everyone else is gone Old Faithful is still here.

Till death do us part!

One night you fell into a deep sleep with me right by your side. I waited patiently while I watched you sleep. I knew you would wake up needing me. Don't you worry, I'm here to stay. I'm not going anywhere.

Till death do us part!

Don't be so bitter, girl. I'm the one who nursed you when you were sick with the flu. You didn't want to go to the hospital, after I convinced you that all you needed was my love and attention and pain and misery that I give you so well. You see, wasn't I right? Don't you feel better? I know what's best for you, my slave.

Till death do us part!

Wow, we've been together a long time now. I vow to never leave your side, your arm, your nose. It's all the same to me.

Till death do us part!

Oh, didn't I tell you? You will do whatever I want and whatever you need to do to keep me. I'll have you sleeping with other men. Heck, you can sleep with anybody, I don't mind. As long as you come home to me. They always do.

Till death do us part!

You foolish girl, why didn't you ask your friends about me before we got together? And I didn't know your family talked about bad guys like me. They warned you. They told you I was no good for you.

Till death do us part!

Oh, didn't I mention when you were in a coma that I was at most of your friends' houses, making them feel good. Yeah, Boo, I've got them on their knees too. You have to admit I'm good.

Till death do us part!

And when I'm not around and you can't find me, you will be in so much pain. No, not emotional pain. We already got that area covered. I'm talking about physical pain. You pitiful girl. You need me, don't you? You can't even wash yourself, lift your arms to do your hair? I'd like to see that trick!

Till death do us part!

Your love for me is no longer a want. It has become a need. You depend on me. You've tried to go for hours without me. See what happens. More pain. You're stuck with me, baby, for life.

Till death do us part!

If you know what's best for you, make sure I'm right there next to you before you fall asleep at night. I know you worry about me not being there when you wake up. You would die if someone took me from you. I don't like causing you pain, but it's what I do best.

Till death do us part!

Okay, now you're talking nonsense again. You can't live without me. You'll just get sick again. You look up to me. So now you wish you never met me? Don't say things like that. It's a little too late for you to want to get rid of me. Besides, who else is willing to put up with all your nonsense? So you're trying to replace me? With who or what? Help? Who's he? I thought I was your HE-RO-IN?

A MATTER OF FACT

BY NELSON FIGUEROA

Life as a cripple
Makes me feel
Like life hinging
On a nipple
Being tendered
With care
Or being pulled
By the hair
Every time we cringe
In fear
Every time
We shed a tear
A piece of us
Is taken or given
To share
Babies know what's
Right—babies know what's
Tight. Give them credit
And don't make them feel
Like a debit
For one day dear
Reader, your time
Will come to be as we are
Once an adult
And twice a baby
Reflect on that
It's a matter
Of fact

HEAVIEST

BY ALLEN RAYMON

What is the heaviest word in the language?

Forsaking all others with the heaviest word
To maintain your equilibrium with the heaviest
Of ornaments. What say you

Pick up the opposite then back to where it all began
Through the clouds, through the mist, an outline
To the wells and a brew for the night

Where, when, why, worry, wink
Lead the way to bring those you love
Lie, lip, lolly, largeness to go to the next level

Find out by testing and touching
You will meet again to take stool, once more music
Surround us with music, hear the sounds from the soul

NIGHTTIME NEIGHBORS

BY DAVID WHITTACRE

It was the middle of the night when Craig was awakened by the distinct sounds of a woman's shrill voice screaming, "No. I said no, and I mean it!" Then he heard the sounds of flesh smacking against flesh and a man's deep voice saying something he couldn't make out. Then again the woman, "Goddamn you! Just get the fuck out of here." There were more sounds of a struggle…slapping and screaming. "Stop. No," and then there was a loud thud as something or someone hit the wall that separated Craig's bedroom from the apartment's bedroom next door. The framed photograph of him and Stephen hanging on the separating wall bounced a couple of times before coming to rest at an angle.

Instinctively Craig reached for the phone, but as he started to dial 911, he hesitated. He put the receiver down. Was it really any business of his what was going on next door? The woman who lived there did have an active sex life. This wasn't the first time he had awoken during the night to hear screams and smacking. But this was different. These were not the sounds of sexual play and climax. Craig was sure someone was getting hurt.

He got out of bed, looking at the clock on the night stand. It was past four AM. He grabbed his jeans from the door knob and wiggled into them, and he headed out his door, leaving it ajar. As he moved towards the neighboring apartment, he could still hear the screams. *What to do?*...He wondered if he himself would be attacked if he interfered. He knocked on the door timidly, but there was no response. He knocked again – harder this time. There was a moment of silence, and then he could hear the sounds of bare feet running on a wooden floor inside the apartment, stopping on the other side of the door. Craig heard two locks unlatch almost simultaneously, *pop, snap!* The door flew open. The woman, his neighbor, was naked – her red hair and arms flying, and her right eye was almost swollen shut. She shot out of her door, grabbing Craig's arm and yelled, "Get outa here! We gotta get outa of here!" He could see a man, his jeans undone and his open shirt flapping behind him as he ran towards the door, and before Craig could say anything, the woman pushed him into his own door, jumped in with him and slammed the door shut. Craig rapidly bolted the locks. His heart was pounding, and he was panting as if he had just run a mile. The woman collapsed on his hallway floor. She was crying hysterically – her back heaving up and down.

The man started pounding on Craig's door, yelling, "You best open up buddy, or I'll break your goddamn door down." He continued to kick and pummel the door.

Craig was frightened, but somewhere up from his gut came this husky, menacing voice, yelling, "You better get the fuck away from my door and out of this goddamn building. The cops'll be here any minute."

"Yeah, well you tell that bitch that this ain't over. And *you* better watch your fuckin' butt, man. If I ever see you on the street, your ass is grass." Then the man could be heard thumping down the stairs.

Craig looked down at the woman. She was sitting on the floor with her arms wrapped around her legs, her forehead resting on her knees. "It's okay. He's gone." He went to his bedroom and took his robe off the back of the door. "Here, put this on." She stood and was shaking so badly that Craig helped with the robe, and he noticed that she had bright red pubic hair shaved into the shape of a heart. *Curious,* he thought. "Your eye looks pretty bad. I'll get some ice."

As she fumbled trying to tie the robe, Craig went into the bathroom, got a fresh wash cloth, dampened it, and then went to the kitchen. He took some ice from the freezer, put it in a plastic zipper bag, hammered it a few times with his wooden meat mallet to crush the ice, and folded the wash cloth around it.

"Here," he said, and handed her the compress. "Are you really okay?" He gave her an assuring touch on the shoulder.

"Yeah, I'm fine. Just a little shaky."

She looked up at him, with tears running down her face, she said, "By the way, my name is Ruth. Ruth Davis." She put out her hand to give Craig a handshake. "What a way to meet, huh? Christ, I can't believe that happened. He seemed so nice at the club. Goddamn fuckin' men!"

"Come and sit down." He guided her into the living room. "I'll make some coffee."

"Great."

Craig busied himself making coffee. Ruth sat on the sofa, clutching the robe at her neck. It almost covered her breasts. She was still trembling. "Are the police really comin'? I don't feel like talkin' to them."

"No. I just said that to scare that guy away." The coffee was starting to drip into the pot.

"Well, that's a relief. On top of everything else tonight, I couldn't face the cops askin' all kinds of personal stuff, like who was the man, and what kind of club it was where I had met him."

These were the kinds of things that Craig himself wanted to ask, but he refrained.

"Are you really okay? I could take you to the emergency room at Roosevelt Hospital. It's just two blocks…"

"No. No emergency rooms! There's nothin' broken – just some bruises." She got up and walked to the mirror hanging over the fireplace. She took the compress away from her eye. "Jesus Christ! Look at this fuckin' shiner. That goddamned bastard!" She lightly pressed her fingers around her swelling eye. Her coppery red hair was a messy mass of curls and waves falling just past her shoulders. She had a pretty face in spite of the eye – high cheek bones, full lips, and there was something very childlike about her. Maybe it was her flawless, pale skin. It certainly wasn't her breasts.

"What do you take in your coffee?"

"Black, with lots of sugar"

Craig handed her a mug of coffee. "You should keep the ice on your eye. It's only going to swell more if you don't."

"And of all the times for this to happen. I'm not gonna be able to work for at least a week. This weekend I'm supposed to be on the main stage!"

"Are you an actress? No one in the audience would notice your eye with some clever stage makeup."

She laughed with a high-pitched squeal. Even her laughter was childlike.

"*My* audience would know if I had a hair growin' outa my ass." She sat down and took a sip of coffee. She noticed Craig looked perplexed.

"You ever hear of 'Show Paradise'? I'm not really an actress – I'm an exotic dancer." She squealed again. It sounded like someone had squeezed a rubber squeak toy. "I'm a stripper."

"Oh." It was the only thing Craig could think of to say.

"That's why I came to New York. You know I'm not really from here." Craig knew that from her accent—*Arkansas* maybe? "Back home there aren't any jobs for exotic dancers. There were beer joints where women stood up on the bar and stripped, but those women were just whores tryin' to drum up business. They couldn't dance. They just wiggled 'round 'til some ol' redneck grabbed 'em, took them out to the parkin' lot, threw them in their pickups with a six-pack, and raced off to the nearest motel. That wasn't for me. No sirree."

"I'd been the best in the girls' gymnastics class, and I knew how to move this body. And I took a couple of years of dance classes in Fayetteville." So Craig had been right about her maybe coming from Arkansas.

"You wanta see one of my moves?" And without Craig being able to answer, she bolted to the end of the long living room, turned to face the opposite wall, took a couple of leaps and did a complete flip in the air, the robe falling off, and came to rest in splits with her hands held high in the air, beaming as if she were on stage. She nonchalantly picked up the robe and put it back on. She didn't seem to be the least bit embarrassed by being naked in front of someone she didn't know. Craig thought, *well, she* is *a stripper after all.*

"Oh. Ouch! That really made my face hurt." She took the compress from where she had been sitting and put it back on her eye. "Once when I was performin', I forgot ta take my spike heels off when I did that move, and when I came outa the flip, I twisted my ankle and flew right off the stage into the laps of three Japanese men sittin' together. They must have thought it was part of the show, 'cause they started laughin' and clappin' and jabberin' in Japanese to each other. I sprained my ankle so bad that it blew up like a balloon. Somehow, I crawled back into the dressin' room and changed into my street clothes, and the two bouncers carried me out to the street and got me a cab. Then when I got to the apartment building, it took me about twenty minutes to slide up the stairs backwards, on my butt, to get up to my apartment. I couldn't perform for three whole weeks after that!"

Craig tried to keep from laughing, imaging her going from stair to stair on her butt, but he was also watching the clock on the mantel. It was a little after five o'clock now. His normal wakeup time was at six, but he thought, *what's one hour of sleep?* He prayed to God that she wasn't about to launch off into anymore about her life's story, but...

"So, six years ago, I got on a Greyhound bus in Fayetteville with two suitcases and headed for New York City. It took three days on that stinky ol' bus to get here. Then I had to find a cheap hotel, and I found one in the Times Square area, and you wouldn't believe this place. The sheets were full of holes, and, in the bathroom, there was only a sink and one of those bidet things. No bathtub. And durin' my first night there I kept hearin' lotsa women gigglin' and men's voices out in the hall, and doors kept openin' and closin' all night long, and the walls were thin, so I knew what was goin' on in the other rooms. On my second day there, I found out that rooms were mostly rented by the hour, and you know what that means. But I was tryin' not to spend much money, and this place was cheap!"

Craig got up and refilled their coffee mugs.

"Thanks," she said. "Anyway, when I started lookin' for an apartment, I was shocked by rent prices, but I didn't have a lot of time before my money would run out, so I took what I could afford. It was an awful place down on Avenue C. Plaster was fallin' off the walls, the linoleum in the kitchen was buckled and had holes in it, some of windows were broken, the bathtub was in the kitchen, there were cockroaches everywhere, and the place was fil-thee!" she exclaimed. "But the worst thing was that the toilet was out in the hall! Can you believe that?"

"I've heard of that sort of thing."

"The other people who used it were *not* clean. I must have gone through a gallon of bleach every week in that water closet. Why do they call it that? My apartment only had two rooms, but the rent was just two seventy-five a month—much less than anything else I'd looked at, so I took it. Then I got a waitress job. I'd worked at a truck stop diner just outside of Fayetteville. That was about the only work experience I had. I was fired from my first wait-ress job here in New York 'cause you had to carry food on big trays. I'd never done that, and I dropped three trays of food. The manager told me not to bother comin' back, so I found a job in a coffee shop. I carried food in my hands and up my arms. That's what I was used ta doin'. So I got on fine there."

"I worked the late shift, and it's a miracle that I didn't get killed in my neighborhood, comin' home at one or two in the mornin'. I had to climb over junkies and drunks just to get up the front steps of the buildin'."

"But I was able to save enough money to get my boob

job. It was hard findin' a doctor who would agree to change my 'B' cups into 'E' cups. So now I have these wonderful 'girls,'" and she joggled her breasts from side to side and squealed with that laugh again. This made Craig uncomfortable. Women's breasts had always made him nervous. And these 'girls' were huge. The size of cantaloupes!

He looked away from the 'girls,' which had fallen out of his robe, and said, "When *I* moved to the city fifteen years ago, I also was hunting for an affordable apartment. A friend of mine had just moved into an apartment on Avenue A. All his friends who knew the city tried to talk him out of it. Anywhere east of Tompkins Square Park looked like London after the blitzkrieg." Ruth didn't know what that meant, but Craig went on... "Some of the tenement buildings were falling down, and a lot of the ones still standing had squatters."

"Squatters?" Ruth asked.

"Yeah. People who lived in abandoned buildings and paid no rent, but they had no heat, no electricity, no phones..."

"Back home, we call 'em hillbillies. Well, anyway," she went on, "ten years ago when I got my apartment there, things were a little better. But not much. It was a neighborhood full of scary thugs, sellin' drugs on the street corners, sleepin' on the steps of the buildings. And I guess the city had torn down a lot of the old empty buildings. You just saw empty lots that were dumpin' grounds for burned-out cars, old kitchen stoves and refrigerators, and big cardboard boxes that people lived in. Can you believe it? And there were rats everywhere. And the stink? The stink was nauseatin'! People even used the lots for bathrooms. I'm so glad I got outa there and got this apartment here."

"Yeah, but that area *is* changing," Craig said. "A lot of New York University students have been moving into that neighborhood, looking for cheap rent and for places that aren't that far from the university, and rents have been going up there. That whole area is becoming a hip place to live now. I have a friend who just moved into that area and he's paying six-fifty a month for three small rooms—in an old tenement building."

"No! Go on...I don't pay much more than that here." She paused for a moment, reached for her coffee, and asked Craig, "Why do they call this area Hell's Kitchen?"

"Well, this used to be a rough neighborhood, and Ninth Avenue was a big, rundown, wholesale food market. Oh...and I don't know if you know this, but the last elevated train ran down Ninth Avenue."

"Elevated train?"

"Yes. A lot of the subways were on tracks *above* the streets, so they called them 'elevated trains'. You had to walk *up* the stairs to get to the platforms. You can still see them in other boroughs. You ever been to Queens?"

"Yeah...Oh...the tracks *are* built above the streets there, but I've never heard them called 'elevated trains'."

"I think the Ninth Avenue elevated train was the last one to be taken out in Manhattan. It was done in the nineteen-fifties." Craig looked at the clock and panicked. It was six-thirty!

"What kinda work do you do?"

"I work at the Met," he said, while thinking of how to politely get Ruth out of his apartment.

"Wow! That's a great museum! I've only been there a couple of times. I don't know much about art. Are you an artist?"

"No. And I don't work at the Metropolitan Museum. I work at the Metropolitan Opera. People refer to it as, 'The Met.' And I'm not a singer either. I take care of the star opera singers when they come to the city to sing at the Met. Sounds like an easy job, but you wouldn't believe how ridiculously demanding those divas can be. Females and males. They don't like their hotel suites; they don't like their limousine drivers, they don't like the restaurants they're taken to…Nothing pleases them, and I have to deal with all their ridiculous needs. My friends at the Met call me the 'Queen of the Divas'."

"Why do they call you that?"

"Well…if you haven't guessed, I'm gay. And one of the slang names for a gay man is 'Queen.'"

"I wondered about that. I know you have a male room-mate, and you only have one bedroom. Ya know?" She paused. "As a matter of fact—I haven't seen your roommate in a long time. He has the dreamiest, big brown eyes with eyelashes I would die for! And he's always so nice. When we would bump into each other in the hall, and I was carryin' sacks of groceries, he would carry them up for me. Did he move out?"

"Uh…no." Craig turned and looked out the window for a few moments. "He died about five months ago."

"Oh, Craig. I'm sorry." She put her hand on his arm. "How long had you two been together?"

"For eight years."

"It's none of my business, but how did he die?"

Craig looked down at his lap and picked a piece of lint off his jeans. "Um…it was AIDS."

Ruth had been in New York long enough to know about gay men and AIDS. A couple of the gay male dancers at the club had died of AIDS.

"You must really miss him."

"Yes, I do. He was the only man whom I ever *really, really* loved. It's funny. In a lot of ways we were very different. He was the one with dark, wavy hair, big brown eyes, as you noticed, and he could walk into a room full of people and start talking to everyone. He had such a warm, easy personality, that everyone was drawn to him immediately. I, on the other hand, was the one with blond hair and blue eyes—the light one. When *I* walked into a room of people, I would try to find a place to sit and not really talk to anyone. Stephen was interested in everyone. I've always been timid and shy. I mean, if a person speaks to me, I'll talk back, and sometimes I find a person interesting and will have a good conversation. But most of the time, I'm just a wall flower."

Ruth found that hard to believe. Craig was very handsome. He must have been six feet tall. He had beautiful, light, almost platinum blond hair, a good body, perfectly white teeth. If he'd been straight, Ruth would certainly go after him. Hell…even knowing that he was gay, she was still attracted to him.

"I always wondered why Stephen was attracted to me. But, as they say, 'opposites attract.'" Ruth saw a tear running down his cheek, and he didn't say anything for a while, and she remained silent.

"Listen, Ruth…I don't want to be rude, but I *have* to start getting ready for work. We have a big star coming in this afternoon. She's the hot soprano in the opera world now, and I have a lot of preparations to finish. She's one of the monster divas who makes life miserable for everyone. Maria Conzarella. I dread her arrival. I have to meet her at Kennedy Airport at three this afternoon. She travels with steamer trunks." Craig chuckled. "It takes one of the *very* long limousines just to get her and all her stuff to the hotel. And…Oh, fuck!" He jumped up from the sofa.

It startled Ruth. "What's wrong?" she asked.

"I forgot to change the Steinway piano in her hotel suite. She always insists on having the 'B' model, instead of the 'L' that we keep there. She says the 'B' is more sonorous and is more suitable to her voice when she does her vocalizing. The 'L' is only one foot shorter than the 'B.' I hope Steinway can make the switch before she gets here. God…I can't believe I forgot."

"Okay. Well let me get outa here and let you get ready. Good luck."

Ruth walked towards the door and Craig followed her into her apartment, saying, "I'll help you check to make sure if that guy really is gone."

They did a quick search. The man was gone, so Craig said, "Bye" as he ran down the hallway to his apartment. He heard Ruth shouting, "Thank you, Craig."

The first thing he did when he closed his door was to make a call to his supervisor at the Met. After a few rings, he realized it was a little early for his supervisor to be there, so he ran to the bedroom, took off his jeans and t-shirt, and raced into the bathroom. He was usually very attentive to shaving and showering. Usually he spent an hour in the bathroom doing his morning rituals. This morning he spent only about twenty minutes. He thought that this must have been a record.

He ran to the phone again and dialed his supervisor, but there was still no answer. He put on all his underclothing and shirt, and chose his cashmere, navy blue suit, and put it on. From the top of his bureau, he snatched all the things he carried in his various pockets. He didn't even attempt tying his tie. He ran into the bathroom and looked into the mirror and said out loud, "Craig, you look like shit!" As he sprayed on some cologne, he grabbed the phone again. This time he got an answer. "Mr. Eppstein, I'm running a little late. There was an emergency in my building that I had to take care of, but I'm on my way now."

Mr. Eppstein replied, "You do know who's coming in today, don't you?"

"Of course I know that bitch," and as soon as he said "bitch," he knew he'd made a faux pas, so he said, "Sorry, I shouldn't have said that."

Mr, Eppstein said, "Well, she is a bitch, but don't ever call her that again."

"Okay. Sorry. I'll be there in about ten or fifteen minutes."

"See that it's no longer than that!"

"Right-o." And he hung up. He skipped down the stairs, hoping it wouldn't take long to find a cab. It was his luck that a woman was getting out of a cab right in front of his building. He grabbed the door before she had time to close it, almost knocking her over, jumped in, slammed the door, and shouted to the driver, "Lincoln Center, and I'm in a real hurry!" And off they sped. As he was trying to button his shirt cuffs and tying his tie, he said over and over to himself, *Steinway, Steinway, Steinway....*

YOUR HONOR

BY RUBY CARRASQUILLO

Hello, Your Honor.

Judge, judge, here comes the fucking judge. You sit up on your high chair thinking you really know me. When you don't know a damn thing about me. You don't know that I have a family and people who love me as I do them.

You expect everyone to just shut up in your fucking courtroom, but damn, don't my tax money pay for you to have that chair? Sometimes I wonder, have you ever really lived or had a good fuck? You seem like you need one.

I understand that I'm a career criminal but I'm not an animal. Don't assume you know me by looking at a Rap Sheet—Ridiculous Appearance Papers.

You will not get into heaven any easier than I.

Have a nice day!

ON 14TH STREET

BY LORRAINE THEODOR

She sits on a bench most days in Union Square Park with a world of history in her eyes. I wondered about her past—is there family? Well, a few days ago I asked her name. "Elizabeth Victoria," she answered rather pensively. A queenly name, I thought.

We spoke for a while and were interrupted now and then by people giving her coins, which she thanked them for. As she turned her gaze back to me, I saw bewilderment in her light colored eyes, and then surprise to see me standing and waiting for her. Slowly and softly Elizabeth started to tell me of her dancing days.

She came from a small town in Arkansas where nothing ever happened, she said. She thought New York City was the place to be and where she was going to make it big. Elizabeth did get a job in the chorus of the top show in town. She loved the city and the city loved her. "I was quite the thing," she said. "Ginger Rogers had nothing on me. The audience loved me and the men spoiled me. Then I met Frank. He told me to stick with him, that he would give me the world. Frank was so handsome and powerful, it seemed like the world was his to give—where money came easily and, I guess, too quickly. I was thrilled when he took me along with him."

After a long pause with eyes that seemed to burn, she said, "I loved that man. We were dynamite together. But you know something lady? We were going too fast. We crashed. And when I looked around, Frank was no longer there, and I just couldn't get back on track…But I'll make it some day."

She got up to walk away. Suddenly she turned and with the most beguiling smile she said, "Lady, come back, 'cause I've got stuff to tell you that will knock your socks off."

I'll be back, because if this lady wants to talk, I'll be listening.

OUT OF THE CHAMBER

BY NELSON FIGUEROA

I have AIDS.
Death looms near.
Basic situations
Take on perverse interpretations.
Strapped down on an MRI sled
Apprehensions, visions of cremation—hell fires—
Form in my pre-procedure
Countdown to God knows
What they are looking for.
I have to trust.
It comes not easily
Suddenly—whoosh!—I'm in
And now the cacophony of
Gear grinding gear and
The raps on the coffin-like structure
Kunk, kunk, kunk
Oh my God a new sound
Distant but familiar
Sounds that could possibly be
But how would I know?
When does one know?
When you hear what I hear
I hear the new sound
The now perverse mind twisting
A lasting impression
Scunk-shah, shuckska-tamp

Shuck-shuck-tamp
A shovel raking, scooping
Up dirt and tamping tired earth
Is what I hear
I see all too painfully clear
It hurts—I see my
Parents' gravestone, all too vivid.
Ramón Enrique and Diana Reyes
Voluminous guilt fills me
I cry hard and long
For no one can see me
I feel no shame
Save that for my own
No one can feel what
My tortured soul feels
The kunks return rhythmic
But I can't move
I can't hold on
Enough! Arrgghh!! I cry out loud
Loud enough to be heard
Above the din, louder than my
Silent fears—enough!
I'm breaking up, I'm crashing down
Out of orbit from another realm
Another plane—suddenly the
Last blast of clicks, raps, kunks
Whish!!----------I'm out!
The light blinds me
I'm incoherent, visibly shaken
I wipe my tears
And thank God
I'm alive
Out of the chamber.

DARK SECRET

BY YVONNE FOLK

I was scared when I went to Jail
I did not know what to do
I was told what to do and what not to do
I was very scared
I did not know anybody that was there
I cried every night I was there
I had no more tears left

JOHNNY

BY JUDY TAYLOR

A black and white picture through a tenement window

Johnny straddles a kitchen chair
A pack of Marlboros rolled up in his t-shirt sleeve
His saxophone rests on one side of the table
                                            while
A spoon and eyedropper lie on the other

From that moment I knew he was doomed

SHE HAS NO CHOICE

BY JIANNA CAINES

She has no choice but to cop

She has no choice
As she goes in and out
Tuned in to her favorite station
As the devil eats her soul during
A commercial
She cries for a savior
And bleeds for an answer
She has no choice

She has no choice but to be premeditated
A high instead of feeling when
Life says to feel
She cops when the hustlers deal

She has no choice because she
Volunteered her freedom for one night,
One hit, and has been stuck
On the shit since

Sweetheart, sadly, really ain't dumb or
Dense but when she needs
Love a hustler sees
Dollars and cents

A hustler ain't got a choice
Her life mixes and crime pays
So I gotta eat
Tough choice but you won't
Hear it in his voice

She has no choice
She goes in and dips out
Feeling what's natural on life's terms
Instead of a premeditated high that holds her
Between a rock and a hard place

Yet no matter the pain
It's like tuning in to her favorite station
While the devil takes her soul

Only she feels what she feels
And only divine intervention can save her
Although her mother made her
She has become a distant stranger

Like the man in front of you on line
Ready to swipe his MetroCard
To get on the train
Who knows where he is going or what
He does at night
Or where he has been

Her mother wonders the same thing
About her daughter

So she prays harder
Until she is all cried out
Divine intervention

A hustler's gotta eat
So he ain't got a choice

It kills the community for the
Life of his family and a few
Other things that blings

A hustler ain't dumb or dense
But when he needs food to cook
Just pay a crooked cop
So he won't look

Crooked cops ain't got a choice
Crooked cops don't give a shit
So they condone cause their sergeant
Is crooked too and to keep silent
Is to keep their home

Now she sees the game
And the shit ain't cute
So she walks the other way
Because today she has a choice

ANOTHER WORLD

BY RUTH JACOBSON

What is it that makes New York so ominous?
Is it the smell of death that seems to be all around?
Or the leaves starting to die on the ground?
"Don't go on that street! It is burning up with
death!"
"Mother leaves children alone."
They die in the flames of a cut electric wire.

I try to smell the clean after a rain.
However, that clean, sharp odor that reminds me of
        the sea is never around in New York.
On the lower east side, it is like Halloween.
There is terror in Halloween,
Ghosts and goblins fly around your head.
It is the symphony of the dead.

I am afraid someone is stealing my soul.
I am afraid someone is stealing my shadow.
The billboards shout their messages of cruel torture.
"Man kills with a hand like a scissors.
Man kills with a knife."
It is always frightening.

What happened to the jolly, red-cheeked boys and
girls who used to stand for Campbell's Soup?

Where have they gone?
Is there a special internet space for goodness?
Can you picture these bright-eyed children maiming
someone?

This is a world that worships mayhem.
A world where nudity is always an option.
A world where nothing is sacred.

Can we get along without gossip columns,
without Baby Loch Ness monsters?
Where people appear in the night like green poison
flowers.

Give me back sanity and love.
They seem to be large bushes…
Bushes that smolder in the night…
People who cry and never laugh or sing.
Can't you bring back another world?

KIM HAS A FUR NOSE

KIM HAS A FUR NOSE, FUR LIKE DOG FUR...

BY CLAUDIA RACIBORSKI, AGE 7

Kim has a fur nose, fur like dog fur.
Fur has a red nose, red like the sunset.
Lala has a cute nose, she is as cute as me.
Pinkie has a nose for friendship, friendship
like me and her.
I will always like Pinkie the best.

HANDS

BY CINDY LEI, AGE 7

My family's hands have rings.
I smell nothing on my family's hands.
My family's hands have nails on them.
Sometimes the nails look like moons.
The rings on my family's hands are beautiful.
Sometimes my mom and my sisters put on nail polish.
Some people's hands are long and some people's hands
      are short.
The rings are shaped like diamonds.
The nail polish is pink and blue.
The hands are very soft.
Some people's hands have spots.
Some people's hands have white skin.
Some people's hands have brown skin.

HAIR

BY ANGELICA MERCHAN, AGE 7

My family's hair is all different,
because my mom's hair is curly,
my dad's hair is thin,
and my sister's hair slides.
They smell like flowers,
sunflowers or daisies.

HAIR

BY TIFANY MERCHAN, AGE 9

Everybody in my family has different hair.
My papa's hair is like a dark black rainbow.
My mama's hair is as straight as a line.
It smells like roses.
Catherine's hair is straight as a side of a book.
It smells like tulips. It is also long.
Angelica's hair is black, short, and straight.
It smells like sunflowers.
Janela's hair is also short and straight. It smells like daisies.

MY FAMILY'S HAIR

BY EMILY PROSTKO, AGE 7

Everybody in my family has different hair. My mom's hair is down. My dad's hair is straight and short. My sister has hair so short it seems like it never grows. It's like sticks. My hair is short but longer than my sister's. My cat's hair is black.

CANDY COLORS

BY JAHNIA T. MARK, AGE 7

Everybody in my
family is a different
color. I am a light
coffee brown. My mother is a light
brown like me. My father is a Hershey dark
chocolate. My grandmother is a very
very light brown and she smells like
caramel. My Aunt Sarah is really
really light like white chocolate. She
fixes everybody's glasses when they're
broken. But she doesn't let me get new
ones.

SKINS OF DIFFERENT TYPES

BY NYLEJAH LAWSON, AGE 11

There are lots of different skin types in my family.
My dad's skin is smooth, and the color of chocolate, like
    a nice Reese's Peanut Butter Cup.
My mom's skin is soft, and the nice smell of perfume like
    a field of daisies.
My sister's skin is hard and tough, and smells like baby
    oil.
My brother's skin is as smooth as new granite, and just
    a little bumpy from his goose bumps!
As for me, it is pretty hard to describe yourself.
But here are a few things I came up with:

Looks like rich dark chocolate,
Not all that smooth.
A bit hairy!
But not tough!
Pretty soft.
And smells like honey or sweet perfume.

THE SUN SHINES ON THIS SIDE OF THE STREET

EAST SIDE OF MANHATTAN

BY LORRAINE THEODOR

Sitting on an old schoolroom chair downtown, on
First Avenue and Eighth street, having a roll and
coffee, looking across the street up to the fourth
floor, the top of the building, my old heart warmed
because I saw some of yesterday. Hanging partly
out of the window, trousers and worn shirt,
perhaps put out to dry. My mind wandered back to
a peaceful time, when our clothes dried with the
sweet smell of sunshine.

Strangely enough, now while the whole world
could be exploding, yesteryear is still here for
some people. The sun shines on this side of the
street with Kurowycky Meat Products downstairs.

WHY THE ART WORLD STOPPED SERVING WINE AN' CHEESE

BY JENNIFER R. TATE

I have lived precariously in this city for many years. But it was the year before last that was the momentous year which brought a significant change to my life as I found a solid purpose in frequently and casually crashing art gallery openings. As a result, I had acquired, basically to a point of obsession, a keen taste for wine an' cheese—the two always together as if a single beautiful unit, as to me they always will be.

Because New York has so many galleries, I became secure in the thought that at least once a week, I could realize the whereabouts of a worthwhile are opening in Soho or Chelsea or Tribeca, at which I could enter surreptitiously (with few exceptions), and indulge my admirable, albeit amateur tastes, for the world's best foreign wines and delectable cheeses (I scorned the lower quality American products), and all at no cost to me except for the physical and psychic energy I expended getting there; and also the price of tokens. I adamantly avoided the midtown galleries, as they often possess an intolerable air of superiority, and their wines are usually much too aged; I am strange that way—I actually like young wines.

The art that I experienced—some of it quite brilliant—
was secondary to, say, a superb Merlot washing down a
tasty thick cube of La Gruyere Swiss. Of course, if the art-
work struck me (I do have some appreciation for the subject), that was indeed an added benefit. But I went to the
galleries that year with the sole intent of having wine an'
cheese, and absolutely nothing else! Although sometimes I
would also have crackers; and I did converse with people so
as to appear less eccentric, and therefore less suspicious.

Other than the "crashings," as I call them, my life was,
and remains to be, pretty dull. I have a few flaky "friends,"
and no love jones to speak of. And, though I have a college degree, I haven't much ambition; I am also somewhat
of an existentialist: why pursue ambition only to have the
capitalists overtake it, annihilate it, in one way or another?
So, I hold a mediocre job working in a Queens sweathouse
where all the day long, fifty or so of us women sew and sew
and sew dainty petit bras, only in pink, a color I abhor.
I am still the only person working there of African and
American descent; all the rest are Chinese. Their fiber-opti-
cally straight, hanging locks are greatly contrasted by my
short, fuzzy, standing hair. Many of the Chinese women
like to touch it, as if I am the exotic one, and comment on
it in their native tongues; consequently, I have picked up
a little Mandarin and two Cantonese words. And for all
this I have become a kind of favorite. But, needless to say,
whenever I would seek out art gallery openings, I would
forget that the randomly placed hodge podge of roads and

buildings known as Queens ever existed.

One particular evening, during that glorious, heady year, I approached a Soho gallery where an artist (I think her name was Betsy Biddo), was showing her fiercely painted surreal canvases of a series she called Gynecological Abstractions; I read a review of the show in the *Village Crier* art column. As I entered, everyone literally stopped conversing, sipping, eating, pointing, kissing cheeks, smiling, and stared at me with the deadest expressions, as if my very presence had, in an instant, taken away all their plastic joy. I froze at the door, stunned by all those gazing dull eyes, and all that eerie silence. I became paranoid. And yet, I remained standing there.

Soon afterward, an older graying gentleman, probably the gallery owner, dressed all in black (as I was), with a crewneck shirt, displaying that familiar appearance of art-related success, calmly approached me with a glass of orange juice propped in his hand. As everyone else continued their lifeless gazing, he said to me slowly, with an affected upper crust inflection, "We alllll knowww who you ahhh.... We know puhfectly well why you ah heuhhh..." I raised one eyebrow. "Yesss," he continued still expressionless, "we know all about you." This mode of intimidation had never taken place before. I grew more paranoid as his voice grew louder. "Youhh that *lusah* who crashes aht gallehreh recepshns!" Naturally, I was offended: I thought, "How dare this insect consider this Brownies and Cub Scouts party the equal of a gallery reception without as much as having the *aroma* of wine an' cheese!" The art work itself belied the puritanical draft that flowed my way, and the contradiction greatly baffled me.

After a calming sigh, the man spoke further, "I'm sahreh young ledeuhhh, but, theuh is no wine *oah* cheese at this gathuhring." I was sufficiently embarrassed. But more so, I was disappointed and frustrated: my mouth had been watering and now my buds would not be satisfied. (Such pain is inexplicable.)

I began shaking all over. And then I blacked out.

Later the next day, as I sat in a cold, minimalist room in the mental health and addiction recovery ward of St. Ides Hospital (which was the most convenient public medical facility to all the galleries I frequented, since I had no health insurance), a psychiatrist by the name of Erma Scyksik, stood over me and told me, with an attractive Baltic accent, that I had gotten there by ambulance after some kind and perceptive person who did not write me off as a "drunk," had discovered my unconscious entity lying on the sidewalk just twenty feet or so from the gallery doors. Apparently the gallery people carried me outside and left me there. (What evil can dwell even within the minds of those most connected to the realm of aesthetics.) Dr. Scyksik dutifully informed me that I had suffered from the denial of my own existence, and that I believed subconsciously that without access to wine an' cheese, the world was an ominous sphere of despair. She was right—I mentioned earlier my existentialist perspective, but I failed to mention its major *Schopenhauer lean*. What I had experienced, Scyksik concluded, was a psychosomatically induced, short-term "cancellation of life"—next to suicide it is the perfect nihilistic gesture.

I had a difficult time convincing the medical staff that I was not an alcoholic or compulsive eater; especially the orderly from Bangladesh fairly new to the English language.

"I'm just a little wine an' cheese obsessed," I grunted to all of them, "that's all, for chrissake."

"Well then I'm sorry," Dr. Scyksik said firmly, before I could tell her that I didn't need any help, "I cannotelpyoo. We haven'T goT a proper treaTmenT prograym seT up for wine and cheese fanaTics. I suggest you avoid galleries altogedzer and find some heldzy substiTuTe for thaT absyurd obsyession of yours. Nurse!...Disharge this one."

I was released.

Immediately, I went home, showered, and put on fresh gallery wear, as I referred to my collection of all-black secondhand clothing. And then I headed back to Soho.

A gallery I was quite familiar with had an opening that evening. I arrived in the area early and waited around the corner for an hour, pacing and shaking, and bumming cigarettes from naively generous passersby. (I was fascinated to discover that most New York smokers prefer the short Marlboro Lights), and asking every ten minutes for the time.

Finally, the moment had come that I would make my inconspicuous entrance, and I practically skipped with joy to the glass doors of the gallery.

Blithely I entered.

Fortunately, the space was filled to capacity. But, my god! I made my way through the tens of humid, chattering bodies, to the other end where the gallery always set up its wine an' cheese table, and saw that there was no wine an' cheese! Or remnants thereof! I was devastated. "Blimey! I can't believe this shit!" I said softly, my anger resorting to the profane. "Oh, Arthur [Schopenhauer]," I yelled into the cacophony of voices, "you were so right: the world is filled with nothing but suffering!..." Various faces turned and looked at me. Saddened and paranoid, I left the gallery.

Along the sidewalk, I blacked out again, and went through the same admittance procedure as before at St. Ides Hospital; I was even assigned Dr. Scyksik again, and again she said, "I cannotelpyoo. Nurse!..." And I was immediately discharged.

My first thought upon leaving St. Ides, was to go to a shop for my own bottle of imported wine, and then go to Gristede's where I could find an abundance of delicious cheeses. But a strange malaise overtook my distraught entity, and I realized that, curiously, I could only enjoy wine an' cheese at art gallery openings.

So, as usual, I crashed several more receptions, in a stretch of three days, in search of satisfying my obsession—but hopelessly. No wine an' cheese was to be found: not in Soho, not in Chelsea, not in Tribeca. I panicked. I thought I'd go mad.

Black out. St. Ides.

Only this time I was turned away at once by Dr. Scyksik as she recognized me while passing through the emergency room on her to the hospital parking lot where she kept her Corvette. I knew about this car because, during my first stay in the hospital, before Scyksik gave up on me completely, telling me I should *not* cancel out, she attempted to convince me that life had a lot to offer, and with a proud smile, proceeded to show me a glossy new Polaroid of her gaudy pink Corvette—it even had a huge red rose painted on the hood. (I was sufficiently repulsed.) It was an eighties model, and didn't suit her middle-aged persona in the least. At this point I realized her interests were superficial, even in medicine, and that I would not want her to care anyway. She had allowed herself to become corrupted by capitalism…I just couldn't have it.

Back at home, I made a semi recovery with the reluctant help of one of my insensitive friends.

Then suddenly, the next evening, after another capital disappointment at a Tribeca opening, a promising idea popped into my weary, suffering mind: "I will try Newark! They have galleries there!"…It wasn't New York but a facsimile thereof, once inside the white wall-planes of art.

I attempted to roll into the Garden State via New Jersey Transit, but was mysteriously—even divinely I would say—not permitted to cross the border: the train had made an emergency stop inside the tunnel beneath the Hudson River, at exactly the point that separates the two rival territories. I even thought I sensed a thick dashed line bobbing up and down in the water, wriggling, and passing through the train carriage as I sat there expecting doom. But this fancy was, no doubt, a result of the delusional state of mind linked to a body denied its need for wine an' cheese. I began to feel weak.

The train returned at top speed to Pennsylvania Station. The engineer quit. We passengers were given fifty-percent refund slips at the busy ticket counter; our checks would be issued at the station in ninety days.

"Tree months!" a Jamaican woman yelled. "Christ! You'd tink we were ohl rich and had ohl day to wet in de steh-shahn!" Had I the energy, I would have said, "right on, sister!" The woman railed some more, her voice trailing off as she walked away from the bustle.

Some days after my pathetic Newark attempt, having miraculously managed to control my obsession for a time, and get some needed rest, I heard from another friend, whom I did not trust, about the latest art world buzz which was soon confirmed in writing in a local arts newspaper: all galleries had eliminated their offerings of wine an' cheese at their openings, and replaced it with orange juice and strawberries. Apparently the "lone crasher" as I came to be called, had upset the entire art world by her "discourteous and insidious presence" as no more than a "slyly dressed wretch, an articulate derelict with no interest in art whatsoever," only an interest in "freeloading, and subverting the true purposefulness and integrity of the art world establishment," as one anal writer expressed it. And sadly, it was true. No curator, artist, or patron—not even their attorneys or accountants—could stand the thought of me or the mention of my new tag.

Nearly losing it completely, I telephoned Japan, Europe, Argentina! Were they still offering wine an' cheese at their openings? NO! They were not. (Then I reproached myself: "Whom the hell are we kidding, sweetie? We can't travel to those places anyway on our piddling seamstress of brassieres wages.") But, I did think: "My god! My reputation has been disseminated all over the globe. I'm a living legend!" And yet, I had been cast out, painfully separated from the realm that contained the very seed of my purpose. I no longer existed—my lifeblood had been poured into the lower left hand quadrant—I had been negated...I began to contemplate suicide.

Then I blacked out again, lying contorted on the floorboards of my teeny-weeny, itty-bitty, nearly empty apartment, cancelled for the next nine hours.

But surprisingly, I woke up without the disturbing shakes; although clearly the desire for wine an' cheese—its taste, its smell, its beautiful refreshing image as it graces the table just before being consumed, surrounded by grapes and crackers and Seltzer (which always reminds me of a painted still-life)—lived strong within me, as it does today.

****

Alas, my life had become duller after that era in history—and indeed world history! One nearly nonexistent consolation was that my cheap, unreliable friends began to simulate art gallery openings in their quarters. They would hang the most hideous bargain basement pictures framed in plastic (birds, flowers, mountains, Jesus), while insensitively charging me half the cost of the wine an' cheese. (I have since then found an immediate sad something to pad my unslaked needs, and divert my mind from thanatopic mediations.)

I also write about my past, which brightens my life a bit. I have even had some publishing success. This account here is included in a literary review; perhaps someone is reading it now. It is an example of how I stave off the malaise and the total self-destruction of my entity.

So, I will go on writing (and sewing and sewing and sewing small-cupped bras), and will always look back over those intoxicating days when I *was* the lone crasher, slipping stealthily into unsuspecting galleries, and partaking of the combination delight composed of two of the world's most exquisite food and drink productions.

I suppose that only my timely death will kill my obsession and allow for the recovery of the golden age of art gallery openings where the eminent gift of wine an' cheese will again be served, gratis, and with kindness....

And now, I must have my glass of Johnnie Walker Red.

A BACKYARD STORY

BY BOB ROSEN

Nothing could grow in the backyard. When Sam Klein bought the house, the rear yard had been overgrown with weeds and sunflowers. He cleared out the wild growth and put up a basketball hoop at one end of the yard. The soil was pounded into cement by the two young brothers who, from the time they could throw a ball, turned the rear lot into their personal arena. Two homemade bases separated by the length of the lot gave the two youngsters plenty of room to speed back and forth, taking longer strides as they grew taller and taller. They became talented enough to venture over to the schoolyard where, after doing a bit of showing off before the regulars, they got picked at the beginnings of the match-up teams. Now their rear yard arena once again returned to a weedy lot. It took only one growing season, and the stray cats were back at hunting down whatever rodents burrowed between the weed stalks.

Leo the iceman had been making deliveries to the Kleins since they bought their house. A block of ice in the nineteen thirties was twenty-five cents, and Sam swore that there was something special about Leo that made the ice blocks last longer than his competitors'. Maybe it was his horse pulling the wagon through the streets of East New York. Many ice vendors had purchased trucks by now, but to Leo this grey stallion was a piece of history that he didn't want to let go of. He knew everyone for miles around, so when Sam Klein's top floor tenant moved, Leo had just the perfect couple for that apartment.

Bruno Magnani had been a custom tailor in his city, Trieste, whose eyesight had been failing rapidly. Bruno had pride in his craft and realized that his skills were fading fast too. It was the right time to take his pension and, with his wife, make the move to America. An international city, almost a separate country, Trieste rubbed shoulders on the west with Italy and on the east with Yugoslavia. The language was a mixture of both, and to no one's surprise, Leo acted as an interpreter between Bruno and Sam. Bruno was a gentleman from the old school, very deferential to Mr. Klein, and through Leo, asked if he could do some work in the backyard.

"That's fine with me," said Sam, and with Leo's help, Bruno set about once again clearing out that rear space. Raking, shoveling, and hoeing, that wild ground once again was free of weeds. Bruno carted fertilizer courtesy of Leo's horse through the basement to the backyard. Now that earth that had been a hardpan of soil once again was ready for a new crop. Bruno planted Mediterranean fig trees, about twenty, in rows down the middle of the yard, and along the fences, tomatoes, peppers, and zucchini. The fig trees bloomed in two growing seasons. Green and purple, shaped like tiny pears, they looked and tasted so different from the dried figs in the grocery. Bruno Magnani may have been losing his eyesight, but not his green thumb or his love of sharing his crops with the visitors who marveled at this oasis he had created.

Bruno died suddenly that winter; his high blood pressure got the best of him. The next growing season came, the earth waiting for the manure and topsoil covering that would mean that spring was coming. Sam Klein wondered if another good soul would come along, maybe another Bruno.

LEAVING CUBA

BY ELIA ZEDEÑO

In that respect, we had it easy. At least a whole lot easier than most others.

My parents had relatives in the United States who were able to claim us. This was back in the days when Castro first took over. He said that anyone who did not wish to stay in Cuba could leave. It was actually a great strategy on his part. Most of the people who left were the ones who would resist him most effectively. He played on the emotions of parents who wanted to free their children. The United States agreed to take Cubans in on the condition that an American citizen/relative would claim and take responsibility for us upon our arrival.

We were scheduled to leave Cuba around 1965 but there was a fire at the records office in our town and our papers were lost. My father always suspected the fire was intentional. Communist officials in my town had always insisted on convincing my father to join The Party. My dad is a charismatic individual whom people tend to follow, and communism needed him to recruit others. The day after the fire, a couple of officials showed up at my house to tell my father that since the papers had burned, he had no choice but to stay and join The Party. They said, "Now you're not going anywhere." My father told them that even if he had to stay in Cuba, he would remain neutral politically.

Fortunately, my father was able to get in touch with his nephew again and the papers were filled out once again. On Sunday afternoon, April 4, 1971, a soldier stopped his motorcycle in front of my house. I was only eleven years old but I knew exactly what it meant. I held my breath. In fact, we all did. All conversation stopped and I could hear the sound of my own heart beating faster and faster. My mother must have noticed. She quickly whispered in my ear to show no emotions. When you deal with malice, it's best to remain dispassionate.

The soldier entered our house as if it was his own. Indeed it was, from this point forward. We were given fifteen minutes to take a few clothing items for the trip. The soldier began to inspect our household items against his list of previously inventoried items; i.e., the iron, my mother's sewing machine, the radio, furniture, etc. If anything from his list was missing, we would be refused passage. In fact, every broken item had to be saved for this moment.

Since my father was well known in our town, a few months earlier word was leaked to him that we may be leaving soon. As a result, my parents had a couple of suitcases ready for the trip. When the soldier was done taking inventory, we left our home. A few minutes later, we left our town and everything we knew behind. I still remember the view of my block from the back of the car. I still feel a knot in my throat when I recall the scene. Saying goodbye is never easy, even when the place you're leaving behind is hell.

We spent a few days traveling by bus. We arrived near the airport in Varadero, a famous beach resort, Wednesday night, April 7, and spent the night at a motel. Our flight was scheduled for the next day. Early next morning we were taken to the airport.

Communists love drama—tragic drama. People were being turned away at random. Families were being split apart. Communists can and will exert their warped power, no questions dared to be asked, no reasons needed. My family was told there was no plane available for us. Others who were scheduled to fly with us said we should wait at the airport. We waited until the next day. Finally, by the grace of God, on Good Friday, April 9, 1971, the Zedeño family of four made it onto an old, raggedy Russian airplane destined to never see Cuba again.

The flight was scary. The airplane huffed and puffed like the little engine that could. To top it all off, there was turbulence. My father had to get out of his seat to calm the other passengers who were on the verge of panicking.

Suddenly, in between the clouds, I caught a glimpse of land. It glistened under the sun and spoke to me of miracles, of dreams and fresh beginnings. I saw buildings and what I figured to be a real airport. Once again I held my breath. My mother must have noticed. She squeezed my hand. She squeezed so tight my fingers went numb, not that it bothered me, for I was already enthralled in the prospect of life, liberty and the pursuit of happiness.

BIBLES AND ENCYCLOPEDIAS

BY ANTHONY HANLEY

In 1956 a non-wealthy American had a choice of four ways of remaining in France, as an alternative to returning to an America he did not wish to return to. Have I constructed my thought correctly? He could teach English in the Berlitz School. He could sell Bibles and/or encyclopedias and thirdly, if he already had a job with an American company. The fourth way was to associate himself with a perverted Brazilian millionaire.

There was a fifth way and, what the hell. I might as well mention it. He could become a *clochard,* or bum, i.e., if he didn't get picked up by the cops and discovered to be non-French.

In that year I was an American, non-wealthy, non-bohemian and non-successful. I didn't want to return to the USA but I was down to seven hundred dollars. The return to the States faced me and I got in touch with the Bible and encyclopedia guy.

I am not at all a salesman. I tried selling frankfurter rolls, men's socks and ladies perfume and stuff. I never sold one frankfurter roll, a pair of socks or perfume or lipstick.

The Bible man met me one Sunday afternoon on the Champs Elysees. There was something weird or shrewd about this fellow. The time and place of meeting was peculiar. But I then was a nice guy or a pushover.

This man—I forget his name or perhaps never knew it—next took me to the tenth floor of a building. We entered a large room, all white except for its floor. In the center of the room were two chairs. The Bible man took one, I sat in the other. Our knees almost touched. This guy I can't describe. Well, in a statistical way I can do something.

He was about thirty, of slight build, well dressed, very well I'd say, from West Virginia or Chicago or maybe Oregon. He sold his books to soldiers of the U.S. Army, at the time in various places in Europe. Me, I was confused and I hardly spoke other than to mumble answers put to me. I was angry or introspective, wondered how the hell I had gotten into this spot.

The man facing me, what did he want? I can't say but after I left him I reviewed the interview and concluded that he wanted to find out something about my sales ability or something of my nature, of the type of guy I was. In eight or ten minutes the farce had ended and I was back on the street.

Within a day or two I had picked up information on Bible and encyclopedia selling. You had to be a hustler and a car would have been needed to get from one Army base to another. Sergeants were the best prospects; privates and officers went for neither encyclopedia nor Bible.

I boozed cautiously in the capital of France. I wondered about the movie studios and jobs dubbing in of English but my wonderings resulted in no action. Brazilian millionaires had no interest for me. I don't know. I'm a guy who likes women: women and girls. That left the Berlitz School and American companies. Of the companies I did not qualify. I did apply at the Berlitz School. They gave me an interview and the school told me they would get in touch with me within two weeks.

The Berlitz School contacted me. Probably because I was a bachelor, they sent me to distant places when a branch had a teacher out sick or for some other cause. I went a couple of times to Versailles, once to Lille and I spent a month or so in Luxembourg. For my first night in that city they put me up in the best hotel. There I slept in the biggest bed I have ever seen. Someone told me a top American general had slept in that bed. Might it have been Eisenhower? Anyway I felt it was the world's biggest and it could have given Eisenhower a few nights' sleep. And might Hitler have dozed in it?

ICONOCLAST

BY RAYE WALKER

Like all who have a bone to pick, it's me
Who can't abide the icons that I see
On that eerie old screen
So what am I to do?
Use a hatchet
Or just fret and stew.

My stew is made from vegan stock,
I don't have to use a bone or two.
Hatchets are not in my utensil box.
I prefer my icons on the wall,
They do what I say, not what I do.
A screen belongs in a movie theatre, that's all.

Old movies on my TV screen's a treat
And my vegan stew tastes better when I eat.
I can even do a dance or two, and then
Exercise my old bones for five or ten.
So I can abide the icons now and then.
I'll hone my hatchet for another fling.
I'm ready to fling the hatchet now
Not at the icons but at that TV show.
I can't abide the sleazy creepy things
They stew up garbage just to pay the fare
Of bones that don't even give a care.
So what am I to do.

So what am I to do?
Buy a hatchet that will cost a few
And get a bone to hack away or two
While the screen images dance
And I stew and prance
Abide with me, please do.

Now icons I see where ere I go
So what am I to do.
Am I to stew and fret
My hatchet to vet
On the screen in front of me yet?
I'll put on a record and
Dance around in my bones.

TIPS FOR AGING

BY WESLEY MAXWELL BAYNES

The hope of everyone is to be born young and die old. This requires good planning and a careful lifestyle.

At what point in your life are you considered as aged? Are there more young periods as opposed to aged years? This is really difficult to determine.

In my opinion, when you are born you are very young and helpless.

At age three years, you would have learnt a lot of skills that are necessary. This is evidence of aging. But you are still considered young.

The aging process continues. Again there is significant change at about thirteen years of age. This is called puberty. If you survive to this age you are into your teenage years. Sometimes these are chaotic years. Again the aging process is in play. You are still considered young.

My advice at this stage is to get along with your family and relatives who usually have your best interests at heart.

At about age forty, you should already have a family of your own. You are expected to be wise and a good parent in raising your family. My advice, be nurturing and under-standing.

After forty it's considered all downhill. Wrinkles set in and you have an old appearance.

My advice: Exercise regularly to keep the flesh taut and resilient.

The anti-aging treatment does help the body to recover. Enjoy life!